Charlotte Mary Yonge

Friarswood Post-Office

Outlook

Charlotte Mary Yonge

Friarswood Post-Office

1. Auflage | ISBN: 978-3-73261-986-3

Erscheinungsort: Paderborn, Deutschland

Erscheinungsjahr: 2018

Outlook Verlag GmbH, Paderborn.

FRIARSWOOD POST-OFFICE

BY

C. M. YONGE,

AUTHOR OF "THE HEIR OF REDCLYFFE"

WITH COLOURED ILLUSTRATIONS

BY

A. G. WALKER

SCULPTOR

LONDON:

WELLS GARDNER, DARTON, & CO., LTD.

3 & 4 PATERNOSTER BUILDINGS, E.C.

AND 44 VICTORIA STREET, WESTMINSTER, S.W.

CHAPTER I—THE STRANGE LAD

'Goodness! If ever I did see such a pig!' said Ellen King, as she mounted the stairs. 'I wouldn't touch him with a pair of tongs!'

'Who?' said a voice from the bedroom.

'Why, that tramper who has just been in to buy a loaf! He is a perfect pig, I declare! I only wonder you did not find of him up here! The police ought to hinder such folk from coming into decent people's shops! There, you may see him now!'

'Is that he upon the bridge—that chap about the size of our Harold?'

'Yes. Did you ever see such a figure? His clothes aren't good enough for a scare-crow—and the dirt, you can't see that from here, but you might sow radishes in it!'

'Oh, he's swinging on the rail, just as I used to do. Put me down, Nelly; I don't want to see any more.' And the eyes filled with tears; there was a working about the thin cheeks and the white lips, and a long sigh came out at last, 'Oh, if I was but like him!'

'Like him! I'd wish something else before I wished that,' said Ellen. 'Don't think about it, Alfred dear; here are Miss Jane's pictures.'

'I don't want the pictures,' said Alfred wearily, as he laid his head down on his white pillow, and shut his eyes because they were hot with tears.

Ellen looked at him very sadly, and the feeling in her own mind was, that he was right, and nothing could make up for the health and strength that she knew her mother feared would never return to him.

There he lay, the fair hair hanging round the white brow with the furrows of pain in it, the purple-veined lids closed over the great bright blue eyes, the long fingers hanging limp and delicate as a lady's, the limbs stretched helplessly on the couch, whither it cost him so much pain to be daily moved. Who would have thought, that not six months ago that poor cripple was the merriest and most active boy in the parish?

The room was not a sad-looking one. There were spotless white dimity curtains round the lattice window; and the little bed, and the walnut of the great chest, and of the doors of the press-bed on which Alfred lay, shone with dark and pale grainings. There was a carpet on the floor, and the chairs had chintz cushions; the walls were as white as snow, and there were pretty china ornaments on the mantel-piece, many little pictures hanging upon the walls, and quite a shelf of books upon the white cloth, laid so carefully on the top of the drawers. A little table beside Alfred held a glass with a few flowers, a cup with some toast and water, a volume of the 'Swiss Family Robinson;' and a large book of prints of animals was on a chair where he could reach it.

A larger table was covered with needle-work, shreds of lining, scissors, tapes, and Ellen's red work-box; and she herself sat beside it, a very nice-looking girl of about seventeen, tall and slim, her lilac dress and white collar fitting beautifully, her black apron sitting nicely to her trim waist, and her light hair shining, like the newly-wound silk of the silk-worm, round her pleasant face; where the large, clear, well-opened blue eyes, and the contrast of white and red on the cheek, were a good deal like poor Alfred's, and gave an air of delicacy.

Their father had been, as their mother said, 'the handsomest coachman who ever drove to St. James's;' but he had driven thither once too often; he had caught his death of cold one bitter day when Lady Jane Selby was obliged to go to a drawing-room, and had gone off in a deep decline fourteen years ago, when the youngest of his five children was not six weeks old.

The Selby family were very kind to Mrs. King, who, besides her husband's claims on them, had been once in service there; and moreover, had nursed Miss Jane, the little heiress, Ellen's foster-sister. By their help she had been able to use her husband's savings in setting up a small shop, where she sold tea, tobacco and snuff, tape, cottons, and such little matters, besides capital bread of her own baking, and various sweet-meats, the best to the taste of her own cooking, the prettiest to the eye brought from Elbury. Oranges too, and apples, shewed their yellow or rosy cheeks at her window in their season; and there was sometimes a side of bacon, displaying under the brown coat the delicate pink stripes bordering the white fat. Of late years one pane of her window had been fitted up with a wooden box, with a slit in it on the outside, and a whole region round it taken up with printed sheets of paper about 'Mails to Gothenburg,—Weekly Post to Vancouver's Island'—and all sorts of places to which the Friarswood people never thought of writing.

Altogether, she throve very well; and she was a good woman, whom every one respected for the pains she took to bring up her children well. The eldest, Charles, had died of consumption soon after his father, and there had been much fear for his sister Matilda; but Lady Jane had contrived to have her taken as maid to a lady who usually spent the winter abroad, and the warm climate had strengthened her health. She was not often at Friarswood; but when she came she looked and spoke like a lady—all the more so as she gave herself no airs, but was quite simple and humble, for she was a very good right-minded young woman, and exceedingly fond of her home and her good mother.

Ellen would have liked to copy Matilda in everything; and as a first step, she went for a year to a dress-maker; but just as this was over, Alfred's illness had begun; and as he wanted constant care and attendance, it was thought better that she should take in work at home. Indeed Alfred was such a darling of hers, that she could not have endured to go away and leave him so ill.

Alfred had been a most lively, joyous boy, with higher spirits than he quite knew what to do with, all fun and good-humour, and yet very troublesome and provoking. He and his brother Harold were the monkeys of the school, and really seemed sometimes as if they *could not* sit still, nor hinder themselves from making faces, and playing tricks; but that was the worst of them—they never told untruths, never did anything mean or unfair, and could always be made sorry when they had been in fault. Their old school-mistress liked them in spite of all the plague they gave her; and they liked her too, though she had tried upon them every punishment she could devise.

Little Miss Jane, the orphan whom the Colonel and Mrs. Selby had left to be brought up by her grandmother, had a great fancy that Alfred should be a page; and as she generally had her own way, he went up to the Grange when he was about thirteen years old, and put on a suit thickly sown with buttons. But ere the gloss of his new jacket had begun to wear off, he had broken four wine-glasses, three cups, and a decanter, all from not knowing where he was going; he had put sugar instead of salt into the salt-cellars at the housekeeper's dining-table, that he might see what she would say; and he had been caught dressing up Miss Jane's Skye terrier in one of the butler's clean cravats; so, though Puck, the aforesaid terrier, liked him better than any other person, Miss Jane not excepted, a regular complaint went up of him to my Lady, and he was sent home. He was abashed, and sorry to have vexed mother and disappointed Miss Jane; but somehow he could not be unhappy when he had Harold to play with him again, and he could halloo as loud as they pleased, and stamp about in the garden, instead of being always in mind to walk softly.

There was the pony too! A new arrangement had just been made, that the Friarswood letters should be fetched from Elbury every morning, and then left at the various houses of the large straggling district that depended on that post-office. All letters from thence must be in the post before five o'clock, at which time they were to be sent in to Elbury. The post-master at Elbury asked if Mrs. King's sons could undertake this; and accordingly she made a great effort, and bought a small shaggy forest pony, whom the boys called

'Peggy,' and loved not much less than their sisters.

It was all very well in the summer to take those two rides in the cool of the morning and evening; but when winter came on, and Alfred had to start for Elbury in the tardy dawn of a frosty morning, or still worse, in the gloom of a wet one, he did not like it at all. He used to ride in looking blue and purple with the chill; and though he went as close to the fire as possible, and steamed like the tea-kettle while he ate his breakfast and his mother sorted the letters, he had not time to warm himself thoroughly before he had to ride off to leave them—two miles further altogether; for besides the bag for the Grange, and all the letters for the Rectory, and for the farmers, there was a young gentlemen's school at a great old lonely house, called Ragglesford, at the end of a very long dreary lane; and many a day Alfred would have given something if those boys' relations would only have been so good as, with one consent, to leave them without letters.

It would not have mattered if Alfred had been a stouter boy; but his mother had always thought he had his poor father's constitution, and therefore wished him to be more in the house; but his idleness had prevented his keeping any such place. It might have been the cold and wet, or, as Alfred thought, it might have been the strain he gave himself one day when he was sliding on the ice and had a fall; but one morning he came in from Elbury very pale, and hobbling, as he said his hip hurt him so much, that Harold must take the letters round for him.

Harold took them that morning, and for many another morning and evening besides; while poor Alfred came from sitting by the fire to being a prisoner up-stairs, only moved now and then from his own bed to lie outside that of his mother, when he could bear it. The doctor came, and did his best; but the disease had thrown itself into the hip joint, and it was but too plain that Alfred must be a great sufferer for a long time, and perhaps a cripple for life. But how long might this life be? His mother dared not think. Alfred himself, poor boy, was always trying with his whole might to believe himself getting better; and Ellen and Harold always fancied him so, when he was not very bad indeed; but for the last fortnight he had been decidedly worse, and his heart and hopes were sinking, though he would not own it to himself, and that and the pain made his spirits fail so, that he had been more inclined to be fretful than any time since his illness had begun.

His view from the window was a pleasant one; and when he was pretty well, afforded him much amusement. The house stood in a neat garden, with green railings between it and the road, over which Alfred could see every one who came and went towards Elbury, and all who had business at the post-office, or at Farmer Shepherd's. Opposite was the farm-yard; and if nothing else was going on, there were always cocks and hens, ducks and turkeys, pigs, cows, or horses, to be seen there; and the cow-milking, or the taking the horses down to the water, the pig-feeding, and the like, were a daily amusement. Sloping down from the farm-yard, the ground led to the river, a smooth clear stream, where the white ducks looked very pretty, swimming, diving, and 'standing tail upwards;' and there was a high-arched bridge over it, where Alfred could get a good view of the carriages that chanced to come by, and had lately seen all the young gentlemen of Ragglesford going home for the summer holidays, making such a whooping and hurrahing, that the place rang again; and beyond, there were beautiful green meadows, with a straight path through them, leading to a stile; and beyond that, woods rose up, and there was a little glimpse of a stately white house peeping through them. Hay-making was going on merrily in the field, under the bright summer sun, and the air was full of the sweet smell of the grass, but there was something sultry and oppressive to the poor boy's feelings; and when he remembered how Farmer Shepherd had called him to lend a hand last year, and how happy he had been tossing the hay, and loading the waggon, a sad sick feeling crept over him; and so it was that the tears rose in his eyes, and he made his sister lay him back on the pillow, for he did not wish to see any more.

Ellen worked and thought, and wanted to entertain him, but could not think how. Presently she burst out, however, 'Oh, Alfred! there's Harold coming running back! There he is, jumping over that hay-cock—not touched the ground once—another—oh! there's Farmer Shepherd coming after him!'

'Hold your tongue,' muttered Alfred moodily, as if each of her words gave him unbearable pain; and he hid his face in the pillow.

Ellen kept silence for ten minutes, and then broke forth again, 'Now then, Alfred, you *will* be glad! There's Miss Jane getting over the stile.'

'I don't want Miss Jane,' grumbled Alfred; and as Ellen sprang up and began smoothing his coverings, collecting her scraps, and tidying the room, already so neat, he growled again, 'What a racket you keep!'

'There, won't you be raised up to see her? She does look so pretty in her new pink muslin, with a double skirt, and her little hat and feather, that came from London; and there's Puck poking in the hay—he's looking for a mouse! And she's showering the hay over him with her parasol! Oh, look, Alfred!' and she was going to lift him up, but he only murmured a cross 'Can't you be quiet?' and she let him alone, but went on talking: 'Ah, there's Puck's little tail wriggling out—hinder-end foremost—here he comes—they are touching their hats to her now, the farmer and all, and she nods just like a little queen! She's got her basket, Alfred. I wonder what she has for you in it! Oh dear, there's that strange boy on the bridge! She won't like that.'

'Why, what would he do to her? He won't bite her,' said Alfred.

'Oh, if he spoke to her, or begged of her, she'd be so frightened! There, he looked at her, and she gave such a start. You little vagabond! I'd like to—'

'Stuff! what could he do to her, with all the hay-field and Farmer Shepherd there to take care of her? What a fuss you do make!' said poor Alfred, who was far too miserable just then to agree with any one, though at almost any other time he would have longed to knock down any strange boy who did but dare to pass Miss Selby without touching his cap; and her visits were in general the very light of his life.

They were considered a great favour; for though old Lady Jane Selby was a good, kind-hearted person, still she had her fancies, and she kept her young grand-daughter like some small jewel, as a thing to be folded up in a case, and never trusted in common. She was afraid to allow her to go about the village, or into the school and cottages, always fancying she might be made ill, or meet with some harm; but Mrs. King being an old servant, whom she knew so well, and the way lying across only two meadows beyond Friarswood Park, the little pet was allowed to go so far to visit her foster-mother, and bring whatever she could devise to cheer the poor sick boy.

Miss Jane, though of the same age as Ellen, and of course with a great deal more learning and accomplishment, had been so little used to help herself, or to manage anything, that she was like one much younger. The sight of the rough stranger on the bridge was really startling to her, and she came across the road and garden as fast as she could without a run; and the first thing the brother and sister heard, was her voice saying rather out of breath and fluttered, 'Oh, what a horrid-looking boy!'

Seeing that Mrs. King was serving some one in the shop, she only nodded to her, and came straight up-stairs. Alfred raised up his head, and beheld the little fairy through the open door, first the head, and the smiling little face and slight figure in the fresh summer dress.

Miss Jane was not thought very pretty by strangers; but that dainty little person, and sweet sunny eyes and merry smile, and shy, kind, gracious ways, were perfect in the eyes of her grandmamma and of Mrs. King and her children, if of nobody else. Alfred, in his present dismal state, only felt vexed at a fresh person coming up to worry him, and make a talking; especially one whose presence was a restraint, so that he could not turn about and make cross answers at his will.

'Well, Alfred, how are you to-day?' said the sweet gay voice, a little subdued.

'Better, Ma'am, thank you,' said Alfred, who always called himself better, whatever he felt; but his voice told the truth better than his words.

'He's had a very bad night, Miss Jane,' said his sister; 'no sleep at all since two o'clock, and he is so low to-day, that I don't know what to do with him.'

Alfred hated nothing so much as to hear that he was low, for it meant that he was cross.

'Poor Alfred!' said the young lady kindly. 'Was it pain that kept you awake?'

'No, Ma'am—not so much—' said the boy.

Miss Jane saw he looked very sad, and hoped to cheer him by opening her basket. 'I've brought you a new book, Alfred. It is "The Cherry-stones." Have you finished the last?'

'No, Ma'am.'

'Did you like it?'

'Yes, Ma'am.'

But it was a very matter-of-course sort of Yes, and disappointed Miss Jane, who thought he would have been charmed with the 'Swiss Family Robinson.'

Ellen spoke: 'Oh yes, Alfred, you know you did like it. I heard you laughing to yourself at Ernest and the shell of soup. And Harold reads that; and 'tis so seldom he will look at a book.'

Jane did not like this quite as well as if Alfred had spoken up more; but she dived into her basket again, and brought out a neat little packet of green leaves, with some strawberries done up in it, and giving a little smile, she made sure that it would be acceptable.

Ellen thanked vehemently, and Alfred gave feeble thanks; but, unluckily, he had so set his mind upon raspberries, that he could not enjoy the thought of anything else. It was a sickly distaste for everything, and Miss Selby saw that he was not as much pleased as she meant him to be; she looked at him wistfully, and, half grieved, half impatient, she longed to know what he would really like, or if he were positively ungrateful. She was very young, and did not know whether it was by his fault or her mistake that she had failed to satisfy him.

Puck had raced up after her, and had come poking and snuffling round Alfred. She would have called him away lest he should be too much for one so weak, but she saw Alfred really did enjoy this: his hand was in the long rough coat, and he was whispering, 'Poor Puck,' and 'Good little doggie;' and the little hairy rummaging creature, with the bright black beads of eyes gleaming out from under his shaggy hair, was doing him more good than her sense and kindness, or Ellen's either.

She turned to the window, and said to Ellen, 'What a wild-looking lad that is on the bridge!'

'Yes, Miss Jane,' said Ellen; 'I was quite afraid he would frighten you.'

'Well, I was surprised,' said Jane; 'I was afraid he might speak to me; but then I knew I was too near friends for harm to come to me;' and she laughed at her own fears. 'How ragged and wretched he looks! Has he been begging?'

'No, Miss Jane; he came into the shop, and bought some bread. He paid for it honestly; but I never did see any one so dirty. And there's Alfred wishing to be like him. I knew you would tell him it is quite wicked, Miss Jane.'

It is not right, I suppose, to wish to be anything but what we are,' said Jane, rather puzzled by the appeal; 'and perhaps that poor beggar-boy would only like to have a nice room, and kind mother and sister, like you, Alfred.'

'I don't say anything against them!' cried the boy vehemently; 'but—but—I'd give anything—anything in the world—to be able to run about again in the hay-field! No, don't talk to me, Ellen, I say—I hate them all when I see them there, and I forced to lie here! I wish the sun would never shine!'

He hid his eyes and ears in the pillow, as if he never wished to see the light again, and would hear nothing. The two girls both stood trembling. Ellen looked at Miss Selby, and she felt that she must say something. But what could she say?

With tears in her eyes she laid hold of Alfred's thin hand and tried to speak, choked by tears. 'Dear Alfred, don't say such dreadful things. You know we are all so sorry for you; but God sent it.'

Alfred gave a groan of utter distress, as if it were no consolation.

'And—and things come to do us good,' continued Miss Jane, the tears starting to her cheeks.

'I don't know what good it can do me to lie here!' cried Alfred.

'Oh, but, Alfred, it must.'

'I tell you,' exclaimed the poor boy, forgetting his manners, so that Ellen stood dismayed, 'it does not do me good! I didn't use to hate Harold, nor to hate everybody.'

'To hate Harold!' said Jane faintly.

'Ay,' said Alfred, 'when I hear him whooping about like mad, and jumping and leaping, and going on like I used to do, and never shall again.'

The tears came thick and fast, and perhaps they did him good.

'But, Alfred,' said Jane, trying to puzzle into the right thing, 'sometimes things are sent to punish us, and then we ought to submit quietly.'

'I don't know what I've done, then,' he cried angrily. 'There have been many worse than I any day, that are well enough now.'

'Oh, Alfred, it is not who is worse, but what one is oneself,' said Jane.

Alfred grunted.

'I wish I knew how to help you,' she said earnestly; 'it is so very sad and hard; and I dare say I should be just as bad myself if I were as ill; but do, pray, Alfred, try to think that nobody sent it but God, and that He must know best.'

Alfred did not seem to take in much comfort, and Jane did not believe she was putting it rightly; but it was time for her to go home, so she said anxiously, 'Good-bye, Alfred; I hope you'll be better next time—and—and —' She bent down and spoke in a very frightened whisper, 'You know when we go to church, we pray you may have patience under your sufferings.'

Then she sprang away, as if ashamed of the sound of her own words; but as she was taking up her basket and wishing Ellen good-bye, she saw that the strange lad had moved nearer the house, and timid little thing as she was, she took out a sixpence, and said, 'Do give him that, and ask him to go away.'

Ellen had no very great fancy for facing the enemy herself, but she made no objection; and looking down-stairs, she saw her brother Harold waiting while his mother stamped the letters, and she called to him, and sent him out to the boy.

He came back in a few moments so much amazed, that she could see the whites all round his eyes.

'He won't have it! He's a rum one that! He says he's no beggar, and that if the young lady would give him work, he'd thank her; but he wants none of her money, and he'll stand where he chooses!'

'Why didn't you lick him?' hallooed out Alfred's voice from his bed. 'Oh! if I—'

'Nonsense, Alfred!' cried Miss Jane, frightened into spirit; 'stand still, Harold! I don't mind him.'

And she put up her parasol, and walked straight out at the house door as bold as a little lioness, going on without looking to the right or left.

'If—' began Harold, clenching his fists—and Alfred raised himself upon his bed with flashing eyes to watch, as the boy had moved nearer, and looked for a moment as if he were going to grin, or say something impudent; but the quiet childish form stepping on so simply and steadily seemed to disarm him, and he shrunk back, left her to trip across the road unmolested, and stood leaning over the rail of the bridge, gazing after her as she crossed the hay-field.

Harold rode off with the letters; and Alfred lay gazing, and wondering what that stranger could be, counting the holes in his garments, and trying to guess at his history.

One good thing was, that Alfred was so much carried out of himself, that he was cheerful all the evening.

CHAPTER II—HAY-MAKING

There was again a sultry night, which brought on so much discomfort and restlessness, that poor Alfred could not sleep. He tried to bear in mind how much he had disturbed his mother the night before, and he checked himself several times when he felt as if he could not bear it any longer without waking her, and to remember his old experience, that do what she would for him, it would be no real relief, and he should only be sorry the next day when he saw her going about her work with a worn face and a head-ache.

Then every now and then Miss Selby's words about being patient came back to him. Sometimes he thought them hard, coming from a being who had never known sickness or sorrow, and wondered how she would feel if laid low as he was; but they would not be put away in that manner, for he knew they were true, and were said by others than Miss Jane, though he had begun to think no phrase so tiresome, hopeless, or provoking. People always told him to be patient when they had no comfort to give him, and did not know what he was suffering. He would not have minded it so much if only he could have got it out of his head. Somehow it would not let him call to his mother, if it was only because very likely all he should get by so doing would be to be again told to be patient. And then came Miss Jane's telling him his illness might be good for him, as if she thought he deserved to be punished. Really that was hard! Who could think he deserved this wearing pain and helplessness, only because he had played tricks on the butler and housekeeper, and now and then laughed at church?

'It is just like Job and his friends,' thought Alfred. 'I don't want her to come and see me any more!'

Poor Alfred! There was a little twinge here. His conscience could not give quite such an account as did that of Job! But he did not like recollecting his own errors better than any of us do, and liked much more to feel himself very hardly used, and greatly to be pitied. Thereupon he opened his lips to call to his mother, but that old thought about patience returned on him; he had mercy on her regular breathing, though it made him quite envious to hear it, and he said to himself that he would let her alone, at least till the next time the clock struck. It would be three o'clock next time. Oh dear, would the night never be over? How often such a round of weary thoughts came again and again can hardly be counted; but, at any rate, poor Alfred was exercising one act of forbearance, and that was so much gain. At last he found, by the increasing light shewing him the shapes of all the pictures, that he must have had a short sleep which had made him miss the clock, and he felt a good deal injured thereby.

However, Mrs. King was too good a nurse not to be awakened by his first movement, and she came to him, gave him some cold tea, and settled his pillow so as to make him more comfortable; and when he begged her to let in a little more air, she went to open the window wider, and relieve the closeness of the little room. She had learnt while living with Lady Jane that night air is not so dangerous as some people fancy; and it was an infinite relief to Alfred when the lattice was thrown back, and the cool breeze came softly in, with the freshness of the dew, and the delicious scent of the hay-field.

Mrs. King stood a moment to look out at the beautiful stillness of early dawn, the trees and meads so gravely calmly quiet, and the silver dew lying white over everything; the tanned hay-cocks rising up all over the field, the morning star and waning moon glowing pale as light of morning spread over the sky. Then a cock crew somewhere at a distance, and Mrs. Shepherd's cock answered him more shrilly close by, and the swallows began to twitter under the eaves.

'It *will* be a fine day, to be sure!' she said. 'The farmer will get in his hay!' and then she stood looking as if something had caught her attention.

'What do you see, Mother?' asked Alfred.

'I was looking what that was under yon hay-cock,' said Mrs. King; 'and I do believe it is some one sleeping there.'

'Ha!' cried Alfred. 'I dare say it is the boy that would not have Miss Jane's sixpence.'

'I'm sure I hope he's after no harm,' said Mrs. King; 'I don't like to have tramps about so near. I hope he means no mischief by the farmer's poultry.'

'He can't be one of that sort, or he wouldn't have refused the money,' said Alfred. 'How nice and cool it must be sleeping in the hay! I'll warrant he doesn't lie awake. I wish I was there!'

'You'll know what to be thankful for one of these days, my poor lad,' said his mother, sighing; then yawning, she said, 'I must go back to bed. Mind you call out, Alfred, if you hear anything like a noise in the farm-yard.'

This notion rather interested Alfred; he began to build up a fine scheme of shouting out and sending Harold to the rescue of the cocks and hens, and how well he would have done it himself a year ago, and pinned the thief, and fastened the door on him. Not that he thought this individual lad at all likely

15

to be a thief, nor did he care much for Farmer Shepherd, who was a hard man and no favourite; but to catch a thief would be a grand feat. And while settling his clever plan, and making some compliments for the magistrate to pay him, Alfred, fanned by the cool breeze, fell into a sound sleep, and did not wake till the sun was high, and all the rest of the house were up and dressed.

That good sleep made him much more able to bear the burden of the day. First, his mother came with the towel and basin, and washed his face and hands; and then he had his little book, and said his prayers; and somehow to-day he felt so much less fractious than usual, that he asked to be taught patience, and not *only* to be made well, as he had hitherto done.

That over, he lay smiling as he waited for his breakfast, and when Ellen brought it to him, he had not one complaint to make, but ate it almost with a relish. 'Is that boy gone?' he asked Ellen, as she tidied the room while he was eating.

'What, the dirty boy? No, there he is, speaking to the farmer. Will he beg of him?'

'Asking for work, more likely.'

'I'd sooner give work to a pig at once,' said Ellen; 'but I do believe he's getting it. I fancy they are short of hands for the hay. Yes, he's pointing into the field. Ay, and he's sending him into the yard.'

'I hope he'll give him some breakfast,' said Alfred. 'Do you know he slept all night on a hay-cock?'

'Yes, so Mother said, just like a dog; and he got up like a dog this morning,— never so much as washed himself at the river. Why, he's coming here! Whatever does he want?'

'The lad?'

'No, the farmer.'

Mr. Shepherd's heavy tread was heard below, and, as Alfred said, Ellen had only to hold her tongue for them be able to hear his loud tones telling Mrs. King that the glass was falling, and his hay in capital order, and his hands short, and asking whether her boy Harold would come and help in the hay-field between the post times. Mrs. King gave a ready answer that the boy would be well pleased, and the farmer promised him his victuals and sixpence for the day. 'Your lass wouldn't like to come too, I suppose, eh?'

Ellen flushed with indignation. She go a hay-making! Her mother was civilly making answer that her daughter was engaged with her sick brother, and besides—had her work for Mrs. Price, which must be finished off. The farmer, saying he had not much expected her, but thought she might like a change from moping over her needle, went off.

Ellen did not feel ready to forgive him for wanting to set her to field-work. There is some difference between being fine and being refined, and in Ellen's station of life it is very difficult to hit the right point. To be refined is to be free from all that is rough, coarse, or ungentle; to be fine, is to affect to be above such things. Now Ellen was really refined in her quietness and maidenly modesty, and there was no need for her to undertake any of those kinds of tasks which, by removing young girls from home shelter, do sometimes help to make them rude and indecorous; but she was *fine*, when she gave herself a little mincing air of contempt, as if she despised the work and those who did it. Lydia Grant, who worked so steadily and kept to herself so modestly, that no one ventured a bold word to her as she tossed her hay, was just as refined as Ellen King behind her white blinds, ay, or as Jane Selby herself in her terraced garden. Refinement is in the mind that loves whatsoever is pure, lovely, and of good report; finery is in disdaining what is homely or humble.

Boys of all degrees are usually, when they are good for anything, the greatest enemies of the finery tending to affectation; and Alfred at once began to make a little fun of his sister, and tell her it would be a famous thing for her, he believed she had quite forgotten how to run, and did not know a rake from a fork when she saw it. He knew she was longing for a ride in the waggon, if she would but own it.

Ellen used to be teased by this kind of joking; but she was too glad to see Alfred well enough so to entertain himself, to think of anything but pleasing him, so she answered good-humouredly that Harold must make hay for them all three to-day, no doubt but he would be pleased enough.

He was heard trotting home at this moment, and whistling as he hitched up the pony at the gate, and ran in with the letter-bag, to snap up his breakfast while the letters were sorted.

'Here, let me have them,' called Alfred, and they were glad he should do it, for he was the quickest of the family at reading handwriting; but he was often too ill to attend to it, and more often the weary fretfulness and languor of his state made him dislike to exert himself, so it was apt to depend on his will or caprice.

'Look sharp, Alf!' hallooed out Harold, rushing up-stairs with the bags in one hand, and his bread-and-butter in the other. 'If you find a letter for that there Ragglesford, I don't know what I shall do to you! I must be back in no time for the hay!'

And he had bounced down-stairs again before Ellen had time to scold him for making riot enough to shake Alfred to pieces. He was a fine tall stout boy, with the same large fully open blue eyes, high colour, white teeth, and light curly hair, as his brother and sister, but he was much more sunburnt. If you saw him with his coat off, he looked as if he had red gloves and a red mask on, so much whiter was his skin where it was covered; and he was very strong for his age, and never had known what illness was. The brothers were very fond of each other, but since Alfred had been laid up, they had often been a great trial to each other—the one seemed as little able to live without making a noise, as the other to endure the noise he made; and the sight of Harold's activity and the sound of his feet and voice, vexed the poor helpless sufferer more than they ought to have done, or than they would had the healthy brother been less thoughtless in the joy of his strength.

To-day, however, all was smooth. Alfred did not feel every tread of those bounding limbs like a shock to his poor diseased frame; and he only laughed as he unlocked the leathern bag, and dealt out the letters, putting all those for the Lady Jane Selby, Miss Selby, and the servants, into their own neat little leathern case with the padlock, and sorting out the rest, with some hope there might be one from Matilda, who was a very good one to write home. There was none from her, but then there was none for Ragglesford, and that was unexpected good luck. If the old housekeeper left in charge had been wicked enough to get her newspaper that day, Alfred felt that in Harold's place he should be sorely tempted to chuck it over the hedge. Ellen looked as if he had talked of murdering her, and truly such a breach of trust would have been a very grievous fault.

'The Reverend—what's his name? the Reverend Marcus Cope, Friarswood, near Elbury,' read Alfred; 'one, two, three letters, and a newspaper. Yes, and this long printed-looking thing. Who is he, Ellen?'

'What did you say?' said Ellen, who was busy shaking her mother's bed, and had not heard at the first moment, but now turned eagerly; 'what did you say his name was?'

'The Reverend Marcus Cope,' repeated Alfred. 'Is that another new parson?'

'Why, did not we tell you what a real beautiful sermon the new clergyman preached on Sunday? Mr. Cope, so that's his name. I wonder if he is come to stay.—Mother,' she ran to the head of the stairs, 'the new clergyman's name is the Reverend Mr. Marcus Cope.'

'He don't live at Ragglesford, I hope!' cried Harold, who regarded any one at the end of that long lane as his natural enemy.

'No, it only says Friarswood,' said Ellen. 'You'll have to find out where he lives, Harold.'

'Pish! it will take me an hour going asking about!' said Harold impatiently. 'He must have his letters left here till he chooses to come for them, if he doesn't know where he lives.'

'No, no, Harold, that won't do,' said Mrs. King. 'You must take the gentleman his letters, and they'll be sure to know at the Park, or at the Rectory, or at the Tankard, where he lodges. Well, it will be a real comfort if he is come to stop.'

So Harold went off with the letters and the pony, and Ellen and her mother exchanged a few words about the gentleman and his last Sunday's sermon, and then Ellen went to dust the shop, and put out the bread, while her mother attended to Alfred's wound, the most painful part of the day to both of them.

It was over, however, and Alfred was resting afterwards when Harold cantered home as hard as the pony could or would go, and came racing up to say, 'I've seen him! He's famous! He stood out in the road and met me, and asked for his letters, and he's to be at the Parsonage, and he asked my name, and then he laughed and said, "Oh! I perceive it is the royal mail!" I didn't know what he was at, but he looked as good-humoured as anything. Halloo! give me my old hat, Nell—that's it! Hurrah! for the hay-waggon! I saw the horses coming out!'

And off he went again full drive; and Alfred did nothing worse than give a little groan.

Ellen had enough to do in wondering about Mr. Cope. News seemed to belong of right to the post-office, and it was odd that he should have preached on Sunday, and now it should be Tuesday, without anything having been heard of him, not even from Miss Jane; but then the young lady had been fluttered by the strange boy, and Alfred had been so fretful, that it might have put everything out of her head.

Friarswood was used to uncertainty about the clergyman. The Rector had fallen into such bad health, that he had long been unable to do anything, and always hoping to get better, he had sent different gentlemen to take the services, first one and then another, or had asked the masters at Ragglesford to help him; but it was all very irregular, and no one had settled down long enough to know the people or do much good in visiting them. My Lady, as they all called Lady Jane, was as sorry as any one could be, and she tried what she could do by paying a very good school-master and mistress, and giving plenty of rewards; but nothing could be like the constant care of a real good clergyman, and the people were all the worse for the want. They had the church to go to, but it was not brought home to them. The Rector had been obliged at last to go abroad, one of the Ragglesford gentlemen had performed the service for the ensuing Sundays, until now there seemed to be a chance that this new clergyman was coming to stay.

This interested Alfred less than his sister. His curiosity was chiefly about the strange lad; and when he was moved to his place by the window he turned his eyes anxiously to make him out in the line of hay-makers, two fields off, as they shook out the grass to give it the day's sunshine. He knew them all, the ten women, with their old straw bonnets poked down over their faces, and deep curtains sewn on behind to guard their necks; the farm men come in from their other work to lend a hand, three or four boys, among whom he could see Harold's white shirt sleeves, and sometimes hear his merry laugh, and he was working next to the figure in brown faded-looking tattered array, which Alfred suspected to belong to the strange boy. So did Ellen. 'Ah!' she said, 'Harold ye scraped acquaintance with that vagabond-looking boy; I wish I had warned him against it, but I suppose he would only have done it all the more.'

'You want to make friends with him yourself, Ellen! We shall have you nodding to him next! You are as curious about him as can be!' said Alfred slyly.

'Me! I never was curious about nothing so insignificant,' said Ellen. 'All I wish is, that that boy may not be running into bad company.'

The hay-fields were like an entertainment on purpose for Alfred all day; he watched the shaking of the brown grass all over the meadows in the morning, and the farmer walking over it, and smelling it, and spying up to guess what would come of the great rolling towers of grey clouds edged with pearly white, soft but dazzling, which varied the intense blue of the sky.

Then he watched all the company sit or lie down on the shady side of the hedge, under the pollard-willows, and Tom Boldre the shuffler and one or two more go into the farm-house, and come out with great yellow-ware with pies in them, and the little sturdy-looking kegs of beer, and two mugs to go round among them all. There was Harold lying down, quite at his ease, close to the strange boy; Alfred knew how much better that dinner would taste to him than the best with the table-cloth neatly spread in his mother's kitchen; and well did Alfred remember how much more enjoyment there was in such a meal as that, than in any one of the dainties that my Lady sent down to tempt his sickly appetite. And what must pies and beer be to the wanderer who had eaten the crust so greedily the day before! Then, after the hour's rest, the hay-makers rose up to rake the hay into beds ready for the waggons. Harold and the stranger were raking opposite to each other, and Alfred could see them talking; and when they came into the nearer hay-field, he saw Harold put up his hand, and point to the open window, as if he were telling the other lad about the sick boy who was lying there.

He was so much absorbed in thus watching, that he did not pay much heed to what interested his mother and sister—the reports which came by every customer about the new clergyman, who, it appeared, had been staying in the next parish till yesterday, when he had moved into the Rectory; and Mrs. Bonham, the butcher's wife, reported that the Rectory servants said he was come to stay till their master came back. All this and much more Mrs. King heard and rehearsed to Ellen, while Alfred lay, sometimes reading the 'Swiss Robinson,' sometimes watching the loading of the wains, as they creaked slowly through the fields, the horses seeming to enjoy the work, among their fragrant provender, as much as the human kind. When five o'clock struck, Harold gave no signs of quitting the scene of action; and Mrs. King, in much anxiety lest the letters should be late, sent Helen to get the pony ready, while she herself went into the field to call the boy.

Very unwilling he was to come—he shook his shoulders, and growled and grumbled, and said he should be in plenty of time, and he wished the post was at the bottom of the sea. Nothing but his mother's orders and the necessity of the case could have made him go at all. At last he walked off, as if he had lead in his feet, muttering that he wished he had not some one to be always after him. Mrs. King looked at the grimy face of his disreputable-looking companion, and wondered whether he had put such things into his head.

Very cross was Harold as he twitched the bridle out of Ellen's hand, threw the strap of the letter-bag round his neck, and gave such a re-echoing switch to the poor pony, that Alfred heard it up-stairs, and started up to call out, 'For shame, Harold!'

Harold was ashamed: he settled himself in the saddle and rode off, but Alfred had not the comfort of knowing that his ill-humour was not being vented upon the poor beast all the way to Elbury. Alfred had given a great deal of his heart to that pony, and it made him feel helpless and indignant to think that it was ill-used. Those tears of which he was ashamed came welling up into his eyes as he lay back on his pillow; but they were better tears than yesterday's—they were not selfish.

'Never mind, Alfy,' said Ellen, 'Harold's not a cruel lad; he'll not go on, if he was cross for a bit. It is all that he's mad after that boy there! I wish mother had never let him go into the hay-field to meet bad company! Depend upon it, that boy has run away out of a Reformatory! Sleeping out at night! I can't think how Farmer Shepherd could encourage him among honest folk!'

'Well, now I think of it, I should not wonder if he had,' said Mrs. King. 'He is the dirtiest boy that ever I did see! Most likely; I wish he may do no mischief to-night!'

Harold came home in better humour, but a fresh vexation awaited him. Mrs. King would not let him go to the hay-home supper in the barn. The men were apt to drink too much and grow riotous; and with her suspicions about his new friend, she thought it better to keep him apart. She was a spirited woman, who would be minded, and Harold knew he must submit, and that he had behaved very ill. Ellen told him too how much Alfred had been distressed about the pony, and though he would not shew her that he cared, it made him go straight up-stairs, and with a somewhat sheepish face, say, 'I say, Alf, the pony's all right. I only gave him one cut to get him off. He'd never go at all if he didn't know his master.'

'He'd go fast enough for my voice,' said Alfred.

'You know I'd never go for to beat him,' continued Harold; 'but it was enough to vex a chap—wasn't it?—to have Mother coming and lugging one off from the carrying, and away from the supper and all. Women always grudge one a bit of fun!'

'Mother never grudged us cricket, nor nothing in reason,' said Alfred. 'Lucky you that could make hay at all! And what made you so taken up with that new boy that Ellen runs on against, and will have it he's a convict?'

'A convict! if Ellen says that again!' cried Harold; 'no more a convict than she is.'

'What is he, then? Where does he come from?'

'His name is Paul Blackthorn,' said Harold; 'and he's the queerest chap I ever came across. Why, he knew no more what to do with a prong than the farmer's old sow till I shewed him.'

'But where did he come from?' repeated Alfred.

'He walked all the way from Piggot's turnpike yesterday,' said Harold. 'He's looking for work.'

'And before that?'

'He'd been in the Union out—oh! somewhere, I forgot where, but it's a name in the Postal Guide.'

'Well, but you've not said who he is,' said Ellen.

'Who? why, I tell you, he's Paul Blackthorn.'

'But I suppose he had a father and mother,' said Ellen.

'No,' said Harold.

'No!' Ellen and Alfred cried out together.

'Not as ever he heard tell of,' said Harold composedly, as if this were quite natural and common.

'And you could go and be raking with him like born brothers there!' said Ellen, in horror.

'D'ye think I'd care for stuff like that?' said Harold. 'Why, he sings—he sings better than Jack Lyte! He's learnt to sing, you know. And he's such a comical fellow! he said Mr. Shepherd was like a big pig on his hind legs; and when Mrs. Shepherd came out to count the scraps after we had done, what does he do but whisper to me to know how long our withered cyder apples had come to life!'

Such talents for amusing others evidently far out-weighed in Harold's consideration such trifling points as fathers, mothers, and respectability. Alfred laughed; but Ellen thought it no laughing matter, and reproved Harold for being wicked enough to hear his betters made game of.

'My betters!' said Harold—'an old skinflint like Farmer Shepherd's old woman?'

'Hush, Harold! I'll tell Mother of you, that I will!' cried Ellen.

'Do then,' said Harold, who knew his sister would do no such thing. She had made the threat too often, and then not kept her word.

She contented herself with saying, 'Well, all I know is, that I'm sure now he has run away out of prison, and is no better than a thief; and if our place isn't broken into before to-morrow morning, and Mother's silver sugar-tongs gone, it will be a mercy. I'm sure I shan't sleep a wink all night.'

Both boys laughed, and Alfred asked why he had not done it last night.

'How should I know?' said Ellen. 'Most likely he wanted to see the way about the place, before he calls the rest of the gang.'

'Take care, Harold! it's a gang coming now,' said Alfred, laughing again. 'All coming on purpose to steal the sugar-tongs!'

'No, I'll tell you what they are come to steal,' said Harold mischievously; 'it's all for Ellen's fine green ivy-leaf brooch that Matilda sent her!'

'I dare say Harold has been and told him everything valuable in the house!' said Ellen.

'I think,' said Alfred gravely, 'it would be a very odd sort of thief to come here, when the farmer's ploughing cup is just by.'

'Yes,' said Harold, 'I'd better have told him of that when I was about it; don't you think so, Nelly?'

'If you go on at this rate,' said Ellen, teased into anger, 'you'll be robbing the post-office yourself some day.'

'Ay! and I'll get Paul Blackthorn to help me,' said the boy. 'Come, Ellen, don't be so foolish; I tell you he's every bit as honest as I am, I'd go bail for him.'

'And I *know* he'll lead you to ruin!' cried Ellen, half crying: 'a boy that comes from nowhere and nobody knows, and sleeps on a hay-cock all night, no better than a mere tramp!'

'What, quarrelling here? 'said Mrs. King, coming up-stairs. 'The lad, I wish him no ill, I'm sure, but he'll be gone by to-morrow, so you may hold your tongues about him, and we'll read our chapter and go to bed.'

Harold's confidence and Ellen's distrust were not much wiser the one than the other. Which was nearest being right?

CHAPTER III—A NEW FRIEND

The post-office was not robbed that night, neither did the silver sugar-tongs disappear, though Paul Blackthorn was no farther off than the hay-loft at Farmer Shepherd's, where he had obtained leave to sleep.

But he did not go away with morning, though the hay-making was over. Ellen saw him sitting perched on the empty waggon, munching his breakfast, and to her great vexation, exchanging nods and grins when Harold rode by for the morning's letters; and afterwards, there was a talk between him and the farmer, which ended in his having a hoe put into his hand, and being next seen in the turnip-field behind the farm.

To make up for the good day, this one was a very bad one with poor Alfred. There was thunder in the air, and if the sultry heat weighed heavily even on the healthy, no wonder it made him faint and exhausted, disposed to self-pity, and terribly impatient and fretful. He was provoked by Ellen's moving about the room, and more provoked by Harold's whistling as he cleaned out the stable; and on the other hand, Harold was petulant at being checked, and vowed there was no living in the house with Alfred making such a work. Moreover, Alfred was restless, and wanted something done for him every moment, interrupting Ellen's work, and calling his mother up from her baking so often for trifles, that she hardly knew how to get through it.

The doctor, Mr. Blunt, came, and he too felt the heat, having spent hours in going his rounds in the closeness and dust. He was a rough man, and his temper did not always hold out; he told Alfred sharply that he would have no whining, and when the boy moaned and winced more than he would have done on a good day, he punished him by not trying to be tender-handed. When Mrs. King said, perhaps a little lengthily, how much the boy had suffered that morning, the doctor, wearied out, no doubt, with people's complaints, cut her short rather rudely, 'Ay, ay, my good woman, I know all that.'

'And can nothing be done, Sir, when he feels so sinking and weak?'

'Sinking—he must feel sinking—nothing to do but to bear it,' said Mr. Blunt gruffly, as he prepared to go. 'Don't keep me now;' and as Alfred held up his hand, and made some complaint of the tightness of the bandage, he answered impatiently, 'I've no time for that, my lad; keep still, and be glad you've nothing worse to complain of.'

'Then you don't think he is getting any better, Sir?' said Mrs. King, keeping close to him. 'I thought he was yesterday, and I wanted to speak to you. My oldest daughter thought if we could get him away to the sea, and—'

'That's all nonsense,' said the hurried doctor; 'don't you spend your money in that way; I tell you nothing ever will do him any good.'

This was at the bottom of the stairs; and Mr. Blunt was off. He was the cleverest doctor for a good way round, and it was not easy to Mrs. King to secure his attendance. Her savings and Matilda's were likely to melt away sadly in paying him, since she was just too well off to be doctored at the parish expense, and he was really a good and upright man, though wanting in softness of manner when he was hurried and teased. If Mrs. King had known that he was in haste to get to a child with a bad burn, she might have thought him less unkind in the short ungentle way in which he dashed her hopes. Alas! there had never been much hope; but she feared that Alfred might have heard, and have been shocked.

Ellen heard plainly enough, and her heart sank. She tried to look at her brother's face, but he had put it out of sight, and spoke not a word; and she only could sit wondering what was the real drift of the cruel words, and whether the doctor meant to give no hope of recovery, or only to dissuade her mother from vainly trying change of air. Her once bright brother always thus! It was a sad thought, and yet she would have been glad to know he would be no worse; and Ellen's heart was praying with all her might that he might have his health and happiness restored to him, and that her mother might be spared this bitter sorrow.

Alfred said nothing about the doctor's visit, but he could eat no dinner, and did not think this so much the fault of his sickly taste, as of his mother's potato-pie; he could not think why she should be so cross as to make that thing, when she knew he hated it; and as to poor Harold, Alfred would hardly let him speak or stir, without ordering Ellen down to tell him not to make such a row.

Ellen was thankful when Harold was fairly hunted out of the house and garden, even though he betook himself to the meadow, where Paul Blackthorn was lying on the grass with his feet kicking in the air, and shewing the skin through his torn shoes. The two lads squatted down on the grass with their heads together. Who could tell what mischief that runaway might be putting into Harold's head, and all because Alfred could not bear with him enough for him to be happy at home?

They were so much engrossed, that it needed a rough call from the farmer to send Paul back to his work when the dinner-hour was over; whereupon

Harold came slowly to his digging again.

Hotter and hotter did it grow, and the grey dull clouds began to gain a yellow lurid light in the distance; there were low growlings of thunder far away, and Ellen left her work unfinished, and forgot how hot she was herself in toiling to fan Alfred, so as to keep him in some little degree cooler, while the more he strove with the heat, the more oppressed and miserable he grew.

Poor fellow! his wretchedness was not so much the heat, as the dim perception of Mr. Blunt's hasty words; he had not heard them fully—he dared not inquire what they had been, and he could not endure to face them—yet the echo of 'nothing will ever do him good,' seemed to ring like a knell in his ears every time he turned his weary head. Nothing do him good! Nothing!
Always these four walls, that little bed, this wasting weary lassitude, this gnawing, throbbing pain, no pony, no running, no shouting, no sense of vigour and health ever again, and perhaps—that terrible perhaps, which made Alfred's very flesh quail, he would not think of; and to drive it away, he found some fresh toil to require of the sister who could not content him, toil as she would.

Slowly the afternoon hours rolled on, one after the other, and Alfred had just been in a pet with the clock for striking four when he wanted it to be five, when the sky grew darker, and one or two heavy drops of rain came plashing down on the thirsty earth.

'The storm is coming at last, and now it will be cooler,' said Ellen, looking out from the window. 'Dear me!' she added, there stopping short.

'What?' asked Alfred. 'What are you gaping at?'

'I declare!' cried Ellen, 'it's the new clergyman! It is Mr. Cope, and he is coming up to the wicket!'

Alfred turned his head with a peevish sound; he was in the dreary mood to resent whatever took off attention from him for a moment.

'A very pleasant-looking gentleman,' commented Ellen, 'and so young! He does not look older than Charles Lawrence! I wonder whether he is coming in, or if it is only to post a letter. Oh! there he is, talking to Mother! There!'

A vivid flash of lightning came over the room at that moment and made them all pause till it was followed up by the deep rumble of the thunder, and then down rushed the rain, plashing and leaping up again, bringing out the delicious scent from the earth, and seeming in one moment to breathe refreshment and relief on the sick boy. His brow was already clearing, as he listened to his mother's tones of welcome, as she was evidently asking the stranger to sit down and wait for the storm to be over, and the cheerful voice that replied to her. He did not scold Ellen for, as usual, making things neat; and whereas, five minutes sooner, he would have hated the notion of any one coming near him, he now only hoped that his mother would bring Mr. Cope up; and presently he heard the well-known creak of the stairs under a manly foot, and his mother's voice saying something about 'a great sufferer, Sir.'

Then came in sight his mother's white cap, and behind her one of the most cheerful lively faces that Alfred had ever beheld. The new Curate looked very little more than a boy, with a nice round fresh rosy face, and curly brown hair, and a quick joyous eye, and regular white teeth when he smiled that merry good-humoured smile. Indeed, he was as young as a deacon could be, and he looked younger. He knocked his tall head against the top of the low doorway as he came into the room, and answered Mrs. King's apologies with a pleasant laugh. Ellen knew her mother would like him the better for his height, for no one since the handsome coachman himself had had to bend his head to get into the room. Alfred liked the looks of him the first moment, and by way of salutation put up one of his weary, white, blue-veined hands to pull his damp forelock; but Mr. Cope, nodding in answer to Ellen's curtsey, took hold of his hand at once, and softening the cheery voice that was so pleasant to hear, said, 'Well, my boy, I hope we shall be good friends. And what's your name?'

'Alfred King, Sir,' was the answer. It really was quite a pleasure not to begin with the old weary subject of being pitied for his illness.

'King Alfred!' said Mr. Cope. 'I met King Harold yesterday. I've got into royal company, it seems!'

Alfred smiled, it was said so drolly; but his mother, who felt a little as if she were being laughed at, said, 'Why, Sir, my brother's name was Alfred; and as to Harold, it was to please Miss Jane's little sister that died—she was quite a little girl then, Sir, but so clever, and she would have him named out of her History of England.'

'Did Miss Selby give you those flowers?' said Mr. Cope, admiring the rose and geranium in the cup on the table.

'Yes, Sir;' and Mrs. King launched out in the praises of Miss Jane and of my Lady, an inexhaustible subject which did not leave Alfred much time to speak, till Mrs. King, seeing the groom from the Park coming with the letter-bag through the rain, asked Mr. Cope to excuse her, and went down-stairs.

'Well, Alfred, I think you are a lucky boy,' he said. 'I was comparing you with a lad I once knew of, who got his spine injured, and is laid up in a little narrow garret, in a back street, with no one to speak to all day. I don't know what he would not give for a sister, and a window like this, and a Miss Jane.'

Alfred smiled, and said, 'Please, Sir, how old is he?'

'About sixteen; a nice stout lad he was, as ever I knew, till his accident; I often used to meet him going about with his master, and thought it was a pleasure to meet such a good-humoured face.'

Alfred ventured to ask his trade, and was told he was being brought up to wait on his father, who was a bricklayer, but that a ladder had fallen with him as he was going up with a heavy load, and he had been taken at once to the hospital. The house on which he was employed belonged to a friend of Mr. Cope, and all in the power of this gentleman had been done for him, but that was not much, for it was one of the families that no one can serve; the father drank, and the mother was forced to be out charing all day, and was so rough a woman, that she could hardly be much comfort to poor Jem when she was at home.

Alfred was quite taken up with the history by this time, and kept looking at Mr. Cope, as if he would eat it up with his eager eyes. Ellen asked compassionately who did for the poor boy all day.

'His mother runs in at dinner-time, if she is not at work too far off, and he has a jug of water and a bit of bread where he can reach them; the door is open generally, so that he can call to some of the other lodgers, but though the house is as full as a bee-hive, often nobody hears him. I believe his great friend is a little school-girl, who comes and sits by him, and reads to him if she can; but she is generally at school, or else minding the children.'

'It must be very lonely,' said Alfred, perceiving for the first time that there could be people worse off than himself; 'but has he no books to read?'

'He was so irregularly sent to school, that he could not read to himself, even if his corner were not so dark, and the window so dingy. My friend gave him a Bible, but he could not get on with it; and his mother, I am sorry to say, pawned it.'

Ellen and Alfred both cried out as if they had never heard of anything so shocking.

'It was grievous,' said Mr. Cope; 'but the poor things did not know the value, and when there was scarcely a morsel of bread in the house, there was cause enough for not judging them hardly, but I don't think Jem would allow it now. He got some of his little friend's easy Scripture lessons and the like, in large print, which he croons over as he lies there alone, till one feels sure that they are working into his heart. The people in the house say that though he has been ill these three years, he has never spoken an ill-tempered word; and if any one pities him, he answers, "It is the Lord," and seems to wish for no change. He lies there between dozing and dreaming and praying, and always seems content.'

'Does he think he shall get well?' said Alfred, who had been listening earnestly.

'Oh no; there is no chance of that; it is an injury past cure. But I suppose that while he bears the Will of God so patiently here, his Heavenly Father makes it up to him in peacefulness of heart now, and the hope of what is to come hereafter.'

Alfred made no answer, but his eyes shewed that he was thinking; and Mr. Cope rose, and looked out of window, as a gleam of sunshine, while the dark cloud lifted up from the north-west, made the trees and fields glow with intense green against the deep grey of the sky, darker than ever from the contrast. Ellen stood up, and Alfred exclaimed, 'Oh Sir, please come again soon!'

'Very soon,' said Mr. Cope good-humouredly; 'but you've not got rid of me yet, the rain is pretty hard still, and I see the beggarmen dancing all down the garden-walk.'

Alfred and Ellen smiled to hear their mother's old word for the drops splashing up again; and Mr. Cope went on:

'The garden looks very much refreshed by this beautiful shower. It is in fine order. Is it the other monarch's charge?'

'Harold's, Sir,' said Ellen. 'Yes, he takes a great pride in it, and so did Alfred when he was well.'

'Ah, I dare say; and it must be pleasant to you to see your brother working in it now. I see him under that shed, and who is that lad with him? They seem to have some good joke together.'

'Oh,' said Ellen, 'Harold likes company, you see, Sir, and will take up with anybody. I wish you could be so good as to speak to him, Sir, for lads of that age don't mind women folk, you see, Sir.'

'What? I hope his majesty does not like bad company?' said Mr. Cope, not at all that he thought lightly of such an evil, but it was his way to speak in that droll manner, especially as Ellen's voice was a little bit peevish.

'Nobody knows no harm of the chap,' said Alfred, provoked at Ellen for what he thought unkindness in setting the clergyman at once on his brother; but Ellen was the more displeased, and exclaimed:

'Nor nobody knows no good. He's a young tramper that hired with Farmer Shepherd yesterday, a regular runaway and reprobate, just out of prison, most likely.'

'Well, I hope not so bad as that,' said Mr. Cope, 'he's not a bad-looking boy; but I dare say you are anxious about your brother. It must be dull for him, to have his companion laid up;—and by the looks of him, I dare say his spirits are sometimes too much for you,' he added, turning to Alfred.

'He does make a terrible racket sometimes,' said Alfred.

'Ay, and I dare say you will try to bear with it, and not drive him out to seek dangerous company,' said Mr. Cope; at which Alfred blushed a little, as he remembered the morning, and that he had never thought of this danger.

Mr. Cope added, 'I think I shall go and talk to those two merry fellows; I must not tire you, my lad, but I will soon come here again;' and he took leave.

Heartily did Ellen exclaim, 'Well, that is a nice gentleman!' and as heartily did Alfred reply. He felt as if a new light had come in on his life, and Mr.

Cope had not said one word about patience.

Ellen expected Mr. Cope to come back and warn her mother against Paul Blackthorn, but she only saw him stand talking to the two lads till he made them both grin again, and then as the rain was over, he walked away; Paul went back to his turnips, and Harold came thundering up-stairs in his great shoes. Alfred was cheerful, and did not mind him now; but Ellen did, and scolded him for the quantity of dirt he was bringing up with him from the moist garden, which was all one steam of sweet smells, as the sun drew up the vapour after the rain.

'If you were coming in, you'd better have come out of the rain, not stood idling there with that good-for-nothing lad. The new minister said he would be after you if you were taking up with bad company.'

'Who told you I was with bad company?' said Harold.

'Why, I could see it! I hope he rebuked you both.'

'He asked us if we could play at cricket—and he asked the pony's name,' said Harold, 'if that's what you call rebuking us!'

'And what did he say to that boy?'

'Oh! he told him he heard he was a stranger here, like himself, and asked how long he'd been here, and where he came from.'

'And what did he say?'

'He said he was from Upperscote Union—come out because he was big enough to keep himself, and come to look for work,' said Harold. 'He's a right good chap, I'll tell you, and I'll bring him up to see Alfy one of these days!'

'Bring up that dirty boy! I should like to see you!' cried Ellen, making *such* a face. 'I don't believe a word of his coming out of the Union. I'm sure he's run away out of gaol, by the look of him!'

'Ellen—Harold—come down to your tea!' called Mrs. King.

So they went down; and presently, while Mrs. King was gone up to give Alfred his tea, there came Mrs. Shepherd bustling across, with her black silk apron thrown over her cap with the crimson gauze ribbons. She wanted a bit of tape, and if there were none in the shop, Harold must match it in Elbury when he took the letters.

Ellen was rather familiar with Mrs. Shepherd, because she made her gowns, and they had some talk about the new clergyman. Mrs. Shepherd did not care for clergymen much; if she had done so, she might not have been so hard with her labourers. She was always afraid of their asking her to subscribe to something or other, so she gave it as her opinion, that she should never think it worth while to listen to such a very young man as that, and she hoped he would not stay; and then she said, 'So your brother was taking up with that come-by-chance lad, I saw. Did he make anything out of him?'

'He fancies him more than I like, or Mother either,' said Ellen. 'He says he's out of Upperscote Union; but he's a thorough impudent one, and owns he's no father nor mother, nor nothing belonging to him. I think it is a deal more likely that he is run away from some reformatory, or prison.'

'That's just what I said to the farmer!' said Mrs. Shepherd. 'I said he was out of some place of that sort. I'm sure it's a sin for the gentlemen to be setting up such places, raising the county rates, and pampering up a set of young rogues to let loose on us. Ay! ay! I'll warrant he's a runaway thief! I told the farmer he'd take him to his sorrow, but you see he is short of hands just now, and the men are so set up and grabbing, I don't know how farmers is to live.'

So Mrs. Shepherd went away grumbling, instead of being thankful for the beautiful crop of hay, safely housed, before the thunder shower which had saved the turnips from the fly.

Ellen might have doubted whether she had done right in helping to give the boy a bad name, but just then in came the ostler from the Tankard with some letters.

'Here!' he said, 'here's one from one of the gentlemen lodging here fishing, to Cayenne. You'll please to see how much there is to pay.'

Ellen looked at her Postal Guide, but she was quite at a fault, and she called up-stairs to Alfred to ask if he knew where she should look for Cayenne. He was rather fond of maps, and knew a good deal of geography for a boy of his age, but he knew nothing about this place, and she was just thinking of sending back the letter, to ask the gentleman where it was, when a voice said:

'Try Guiana, or else South America.'

She looked up, and there were Paul's dirty face and dirtier elbows, leaning over the half-door of the shop.

'Why, how do you know?' she said, starting back.

'I learnt at school, Cayenne, capital of French Guiana.' Sure enough Cayenne had Guiana to it in her list, and the price was found out.

But when this learned geographer advanced into the shop, and asked for a loaf, what a hand and what a sleeve did he stretch out! Ellen scarcely liked to touch his money, and felt all her disgust revive. But, for all that, and for all her fear of Harold's running into mischief, what business had she to set it about that the stranger was an escaped convict?

Meanwhile, Alfred had plenty of food for dreaming over his fellow sufferer. It really seemed to quiet him to think of another in the same case, and how many questions he longed to have asked Mr. Cope! He wanted to know whether it came easier to Jem to be patient than to himself; whether he suffered as much wearing pain; whether he grieved over the last hope of using his limbs; and above all, the question he knew he never could bear to ask, whether Jem had the dread of death to scare his thoughts, though never confessed to himself.

He longed for Mr. Cope's next visit, and felt strongly drawn towards that thought of Jem, yet ashamed to think of himself as so much less patient and submissive; so little able to take comfort in what seemed to soothe Jem, that it was the Lord's doing. Could Jem think he had been a wicked boy, and take it as punishment?

CHAPTER IV—PAUL BLACKTHORN

'I say,' cried Harold, running up into his brother's room, as soon as he had put away the pony, 'do you know whether Paul is gone?'

'It is always Paul, Paul!' exclaimed Ellen; 'I'm sure I hope he is.'

'But why do you think he would be?' asked Alfred.

'Oh, didn't you hear? He knows no more than a baby about anything, and so he turned the cows into Darnel meadow, and never put the hurdle to stop the gap—never thinking they could get down the bank; so the farmer found them in the barley, and if he did not run out against him downright shameful—though Paul up and told him the truth, that 'twas nobody else that did it.'

'What, and turned him off?'

'Well, that's what I want to know,' said Harold, going on with his tea. 'Paul said to me he didn't know how he could stand the like of that—and yet he didn't like to be off—he'd taken a fancy to the place, you see, and there's me, and there's old Cæsar—and so he said he wouldn't go unless the farmer sent him off when he came to be paid this evening—and old Skinflint has got him so cheap, I don't think he will.'

'For shame, Harold; don't call names!'

'Well, there he is,' said Alfred, pointing into the farm-yard, towards the hay-loft door. This was over the cow-house in the gable end; and in the dark opening sat Paul, his feet on the top step of the ladder, and Cæsar, the yard-dog, lying by his side, his white paws hanging down over the edge, his sharp white muzzle and grey prick ears turned towards his friend, and his eyes casting such appealing looks, that he was getting more of the hunch of bread than probably Paul could well spare.

'How has he ever got the dog up the ladder?' cried Harold.

'Well!' said Mrs. King, 'I declare he looks like a picture I have seen—'

'Well, to be sure! who would go for to draw a picture of the like of that!' exclaimed Ellen, pausing as she put on her things to carry home some work.

'It was a picture of a Spanish beggar-boy,' said Mrs. King; 'and the housekeeper at Castlefort used to say that the old lord—that's Lady Jane's brother—had given six hundred pounds for it.'

Ellen set out on her walk with a sound of wonder quite beyond words. Six hundred pounds for a picture like Paul Blackthorn! She did not know that so poor and feeble are man's attempts to imitate the daily forms and colourings fresh from the Divine Hand, that a likeness of the very commonest sight, if represented with something of its true spirit and life, wins a strange value, especially if the work of the great master-artists of many years ago.

And even the painter Murillo himself, though he might pleasantly recall on his canvas the notion of the bright-eyed, olive-tinted lad, resting after the toil of the day, could never have rendered the free lazy smile on his face, nor the gleam of the dog's wistful eyes and quiver of its eager ears, far less the glow of setting sunlight that shed over all that warm, clear, ruddy light, so full of rest and cheerfulness, beautifying, as it hid, so many common things: the thatched roof of the barn, the crested hayrick close beside it; the waggons, all red and blue, that had brought it home, and were led to rest, the horses drooping their meek heads as they cooled their feet among the weed in the dark pond;—the ducks moving, with low contented quacks and quickly-wagging tails, in one long single file to their evening foraging in the dewy meadows; the spruce younger poultry pecking over the yard, staying up a little later than their elders to enjoy a few leavings in peace, free from the persecutions of the cross old king of the dung-hill;—all this left in shade, while the ruddy light had mounted to the roofs, gave brilliance to every round tuft of moss, and gleamed on the sober foliage of the old spreading walnut tree.

'Poor lad,' said Mrs. King, 'it seems a pity he should come to such a rough life, when he seems to have got such an education! I hope he is not run away from anywhere.'

'You're as bad as Ellen, mother,' cried Harold, 'who will have it that he's out of prison.'

'No, not that,' said Mrs. King; 'but it did cross me whether he could have run away from school, and if his friends were in trouble for him.'

'He never had any friends,' said Harold, 'nor he never ran away. He's nothing but a foundling. They picked him up under a blackthorn bush when he was a baby, with nothing but a bit of an old plaid shawl round him.'

'Did they ever know who he belonged to?' asked Alfred.

'Never; nor he doesn't care if they don't, for sure they could be no credit to him; but they that found him put him into the Union, and there an old woman, that they called Granny Moll, took to him. She had but one eye, he says; but, Mother, I do believe he never had another friend like her, for he got to pulling up the bits of grass, and was near crying when he said she was dead and gone, and then he didn't care for nothing.'

'But who taught him about Cayenne?' asked Alfred.

'Oh, that was the Union School. All the children went to school, and they had
a terrible sharp master, who used to cut them over the head quite cruel, and
was sent away at last for being such a savage; but Paul being always there,
and having nothing else to do, you see, got on ever so far, and can work sums
in his head downright wonderful. There came an inspector once who praised
him up, and said he'd recommend him to a place where he'd be taught to be a
school-master, if any one would pay the cost; but the guardians wouldn't hear
of it at no price, and were quite spiteful to find he was a good scholar, for fear,
I suppose, that he'd know more than they.'

'Hush, hush, Harold,' said his mother; 'wait till you have to pay the rates
before you run out against the guardians.'

'What do you mean, Mother?'

'Why, don't you see, the guardians have their duties to those who pay the
rates, as well as those that have parish pay. What they have to do, is to mind
that nobody starves, or the like; and their means comes out of the rates, out of
my pocket, and the like of me, as well as my Lady's and all the rich. Well,
whatever they might like to do, it would not be serving us fairly to take more
than was a bare necessity from us, to send your Master Paul and the like of
him to a fine school. 'Tis for them to be just, and other folk to be generous
with what's their own.'

'Mother talks as if she was a guardian herself!' said Alfred in his funny way.

'Ah, the collector's going his rounds,' responded Harold; and Mrs. King
laughed good-humouredly, always glad to see her sick boy able to enjoy
himself; but she sighed, saying, 'Ay, and ill can I spare it, though thanks be to
God that I've been as yet of them that pay, and not of them that receive.'

'Go on the parish! Mother, what are you thinking of?' cried both sons
indignantly.

Poor Mrs. King was thinking of the long winter, and the heavy doctor's bill,
and feeling that, after all, suffering and humbling might not be so very far off;
but she was too cheerful and full of trust to dwell on the thought, so she
smiled and said, 'I only said I was thankful, boys, for the mercy that has kept
us up. Go on now, Harold; what about the boy?'

'Why, I don't know that he'd have gone if they had paid his expenses ever so
much,' said Harold, 'for he's got a great spirit of his own, and wouldn't be
beholden to any one, he said, now he could keep himself—he'd had quite

enough of the parish and its keep; so he said he'd go on the tramp till he got work; and they let him out of the Union with just the clothes to his back, and a shilling in his pocket. 'Twas the first time he had ever been let out of bounds since he was picked up under the tree; and he said no one ever would guess the pleasure it was to have nobody to order him here and there, and no bounds round him; and he quite hated the notion of getting inside walls again, as if it was a prison.'

'Oh, I know! I can fancy that!' cried Alfred, raising himself and panting; 'and where did he go first?'

'First, he only wanted to get as far from Upperscote as ever he could, so he walked on; I can't say how he lived, but he didn't beg; he got a job here and a job there; but there are not so many things he knows the knack of, having been at school all his life. Once he took up with a man that sold salt, to draw his cart for him, but the man swore at him so awfully he could not bear it, and beat him too, so he left him, and he had lived terrible hard for about a month before he came here! So you see, Mother, there's not one bit of harm in him; he's a right good scholar, and never says a bad word, nor has no love for drink; so you won't be like Ellen, and be always at me for going near him?'

'You're getting a big boy, Harold, and it is lonely for you,' said Mrs. King reluctantly; 'and if the lad is a good lad I'd not cast up his misfortune against him; but I must say, I should think better of him if he would keep himself a little bit cleaner and more decent, so as he could go to church.'

Harold made a very queer face, and said, 'How is he to do it up in the hay-loft, Mother? and he ha'n't got enough to pay for lodgings, nor for washing, nor to change.'

'The river is cheap enough,' said Alfred. 'Do you remember when we used to bathe together, Harold, and go after the minnows?'

'Ay, but he don't know how; and then they did plague him so in the Union, that he's got to hate the very name of washing—scrubbing them over and cutting their hair as if they were in gaol.'

'Poor boy! he is terribly forsaken,' said Mrs. King compassionately.

'You may say that!' returned Harold; 'why, he's never so much as seen how folks live at home, and wanted to know if you were most like old Moll or the master of the Union!'

Alfred went into such a fit of laughter as almost hurt him; but Mrs. King felt the more pitiful and tender towards the poor deserted orphan, who could not even understand what a mother was like, and the tears came into her eyes, as she said, 'Well, I'm glad he's not a bad boy. I hope he thinks of the Father and the Home that he has above. I say, Harold, against next Sunday I'll look out Alfred's oldest shirt for him to put on, and you might bring me his to wash, only mind you soak it well in the river first.'

Harold quite flushed with gratitude for his mother's kindness, for he knew it was no small effort in one so scrupulously and delicately clean, and with so much work on her hands; but Mrs. King was one who did her alms by her trouble when she had nothing else to give. Alfred smiled and said he wondered what Ellen would say; and almost at the same moment Harold shot down-stairs, and was presently seen standing upon Paul's ladder talking to him; then Paul rose up as though to come down, and there was much fun going on, as to how Cæsar was to be got down; for, as every one knows, a dog can mount a ladder far better than he can descend; and poor Cæsar stretched out his white paw, looked down, seemed to turn giddy, whined, and looked earnestly at his friends till they took pity on him and lifted him down between them, stretching out his legs to their full length, like a live hand-barrow.

A few seconds more, and there was a great trampling of feet, and then in walked Harold, exclaiming, 'Here he is!' And there he stood, shy and sheepish, with rusty black shag by way of hair, keen dark beads of eyes, and very white teeth; but all the rest, face, hands, jacket, trousers, shoes, and all, of darker or lighter shades of olive-brown; and as to the rents, one would be sorry to have to count them; mending them would have been a thing impossible. What a difference from the pure whiteness of everything around Alfred! the soft pink of the flush of surprise on his delicate cheek, and the wavy shine on his light hair. A few months ago, Alfred would have been as ready as his brother to take that sturdy hand, marbled as it was with dirt, and would have heeded all drawbacks quite as little; but sickness had changed him much, and Paul was hardly beside his couch before the colour fleeted away from his cheek, and his eye turned to his mother in such distress, that she was obliged to make a sign to Harold in such haste that it looked like anger, and to mutter something about his being taken worse. And while she was holding the smelling salts to him, and sprinkling vinegar over his couch, they heard the two boys' voices loud under the window, Paul saying he should never come there again, and Harold something about people being squeamish and fine.

It hurt Alfred, and he burst out, almost crying, 'Mother! Mother, now isn't that too bad!'

'It is very thoughtless,' said Mrs. King sorrowfully; 'but you know everybody has their feelings, Alfred, and I am sorry it happened so.'

'I'm sure I couldn't help it,' said Alfred, as if his mother were turning against him. 'Harold had better have brought up the farmer's whole stable at once!'

'When you were well, you did not think of such things any more than he does.'

Alfred grunted. He could not believe that; and he did not feel gently when his brother shewed any want of consideration; but his mother thought he would only grow crosser by dwelling on the unlucky subject, so she advised him to lie still and rest before his being moved to bed, and went down herself to finish some ironing.

Presently Alfred saw the Curate coming over the bridge with quick long steps, and this brought to his mind that he had been wishing to hear more of the poor crippled boy. He watched eagerly, and was pleased to see Mr. Cope turn in at the wicket, and presently the tread upon the stairs was heard, and the high head was lowered at the door.

'Good evening, Alfred; your mother told me it would not disturb you if I came up alone;' and he began to inquire into his amusements and occupations, till Alfred became quite at home with him, and at ease, and ventured to ask, 'If you please, Sir, do you ever hear about Jem now?' and as Mr. Cope looked puzzled, 'the boy you told me of, Sir, that fell off the scaffold.'

'Oh, the boy at Liverpool! No, I only saw him once when I was staying with my cousin; but I will ask after him if you wish to hear.'

'Thank you, Sir. I wanted to know if he had been a bad boy.'

'That I cannot tell. Why do you wish to know? Was it because he had such an affliction?'

'Yes, Sir.'

'I don't think that is quite the way to look at troubles,' said Mr. Cope. 'I should think his accident had been a great blessing to him, if it took him out of temptation, and led him to think more of God.'

'But isn't it punishment?' said Alfred, not able to get any farther; but Mr. Cope felt that he was thinking of himself more than of Jem.

'All our sufferings in this life come as punishment of sin,' he said. 'If there had been no sin, there would have been no pain; and whatever we have to bear in this life is no more than is our due, whatever it may be.'

'Every one is sinful,' said Alfred slowly; 'but why have some more to bear than others that may be much worse?'

'Did you never think it hard to be kept strictly, and punished by your good mother?'

Alfred answered rather fretfully, 'But if it is good to be punished, why ain't all alike?'

'God in His infinite wisdom sees the treatment that each particular nature needs. Some can be better trained by joy, and some by grief; some may be more likely to come right by being left in active health; others, by being laid low, and having their faults brought to mind.'

Alfred did not quite choose to take this in, and his answer was half sulky:

'Bad boys are quite well!'

'And a reckoning will be asked of them. Do not think of other boys. Think over your past life, of which I know nothing, and see whether you can believe, after real looking into it, that you have done nothing to deserve God's displeasure. There are other more comforting ways of bringing joy out of pain; but of this I am sure, that none will come home to us till we own from the bottom of our heart, that whatever we suffer in this life, we suffer most justly for the punishment of our sins. God bless and help you, my poor boy. Good night.'

With these words he went down-stairs, for well he knew that while Alfred went on to justify himself, no peace nor joy could come to him, and he thought it best to leave the words to work in, praying in his heart that they might do so, and help the boy to humility and submission.

Finding Mrs. King in her kitchen, he paused and said, 'We shall have a Confirmation in the spring, Mrs. King; shall not you have some candidates for me?'

'My daughter will be very glad, thank you, Sir; she is near to seventeen, and a very good girl to me. And Harold, he is but fourteen—would he be old enough, Sir?'

'I believe the Bishop accepts boys as young; and he might be started in life before another opportunity.'

'Well, Sir, he shall come to you, and I hope you won't think him too idle and thoughtless. He's a good-hearted boy, Sir; but it is a charge when a lad has no father to check him.'

'Indeed it is, Mrs. King; but I think you must have done your best.'

'I hope I have, Sir,' she said sadly; 'I've tried, but my ability is not much, and he is a lively lad, and I'm sometimes afraid to be too strict with him.'

'If you have taught him to keep himself in order, that's the great thing, Mrs. King; if he has sound principles, and honours you, I would hope much for him.'

'And, Sir, that boy he has taken a fancy to; he is a poor lost lad who never had a home, but Harold says he has been well taught, and he might take heed to you.'

'Thank you, Mrs. King; I will certainly try to speak to him. You said nothing of Alfred; do you think he will not be well enough?'

'Ah! Sir,' she said in her low subdued voice, 'my mind misgives me that it is not for Confirmation that you will be preparing him.'

Mr. Cope started. He had seen little of illness, and had not thought of this. 'Indeed! does the doctor think so ill of him? Do not these cases often partially recover?'

'I don't know, Sir; Mr. Blunt does not give much account of him,' and her voice grew lower and lower; 'I've seen that look in his father's and his brother's face.'

She hid her face in her handkerchief as if overpowered, but looked up with the meek look of resignation, as Mr. Cope said in a broken voice, 'I had not expected—you had been much tried.'

'Yes, Sir. The Will of the Lord be done,' she said, as if willing to turn aside from the dark side of the sorrow that lay in wait for her; 'but I'm thankful you are come to help my poor boy now—he frets over his trouble, as is natural, and I'm afraid he should offend, and I'm no scholar to know how to help him.'

'You can help him by what is better than scholarship,' said Mr. Cope; and he shook her hand warmly, and went away, feeling what a difference there was in the ways of meeting affliction.

CHAPTER V—AN UNWELCOME VISITOR

'The axe is laid to the root of the tree,' was said by the Great Messenger, when the new and better Covenant was coming to pierce, try, and search into, the hearts of men.

Something like this always happens, in some measure, whenever closer, clearer, and more stringent views of faith and of practice are brought home to Christians. They do not always take well the finding that more is required of them than they have hitherto fancied needful; and there are many who wince and murmur at the sharp piercing of the weapon which tries their very hearts; they try to escape from it, and to forget the disease that it has touched, and at first, often grow worse rather than better. Well is it for them if they return while yet there is time, before blindness have come over their eyes, and hardness over their heart.

Perhaps this was the true history of much that grieved poor Mrs. King, and distressed Ellen, during the remainder of the summer. Anxious as Mrs. King had been to bring her sons up in the right way, there was something in Mr. Cope's manner of talking to them that brought things closer home to them, partly from their being put in a new light, and partly from his being a man, and speaking with a different kind of authority.

Alfred did not like his last conversation—it was little more than his mother and Miss Selby had said—but then he had managed to throw it off, and he wanted to do so again. It was pleasanter to him to think himself hardly treated, than to look right in the face at all his faults; he knew it was of no use to say he had none, so he lumped them all up by calling himself a sinful creature, like every one else; and thus never felt the weight of them at all, because he never thought what they were.

And yet, because Mr. Cope's words had made him uneasy, he could not rest in this state; he was out of temper whenever the Curate's name was spoken, and accused Ellen of bothering about him as much as Harold did about Paul Blackthorn; and if he came to see him, he made himself sullen, and would not talk, sometimes seeming oppressed and tired, and unable to bear any one's presence, sometimes leaving Ellen to do all the answering, dreading nothing so much as being left alone with the clergyman. Mr. Cope had offered to read prayers with him, and he could not refuse; but he was more apt to be thinking that it was tiresome, than trying to enter into what, poor foolish boy, would have been his best comfort.

To say he was cross when Mr. Cope was there, would be saying much too little; there was scarcely any time when he was not cross; he was hardly civil even to Miss Jane, so that she began to think it was unpleasant to him to have her there; and if she were a week without calling, he grumbled hard thoughts about fine people; he was fretful and impatient with the doctor; and as to those of whom he had no fears, he would have been quite intolerable, had they loved him less, or had less pity on his suffering.

He never was pleased with anything; teased his mother half the night, and drove Ellen about all day. She, good girl, never said one word of impatience, but bore it all with the sweetest good humour; but her mother now and then spoke severely for Alfred's own good, and then he made himself more miserable than ever, and thought she was unkind and harsh, and that he was very much to be pitied for having a mother who could not bear with her poor sick boy. He was treating his mother as he was treating his Father in Heaven.

How Harold fared with him may easily be guessed—how the poor boy could hardly speak or step without being moaned at, till he was almost turned out of his own house; and his mother did not know what to do, for Alfred was really very ill, and fretting made him worse, and nothing could be so bad for his brother as being driven out from home, to spend the long summer evenings as he could.

Ellen would have been thankful now, had Paul Blackthorn been the worst company into which Harold fell. Not that Paul was a bit cleaner; on the contrary, each day could not fail to make him worse, till, as Ellen had once said, you might almost grow a crop of radishes upon his shoulders.

Mrs. King's kind offer of washing his shirt had come to nothing. She asked Harold about it, and had for answer, 'Do you think he would, after the way you served him?'

Either he was affronted, or he was ashamed of her seeing his rags, or, what was not quite impossible, there was no shirt at all in the case; and he had a sturdy sort of independence about him, that made him always turn surly at any notion of anything being done for him for charity.

How or why he stayed on with the farmer was hard to guess, for he had very scanty pay, and rough usage; the farmer did not like him; the farmer's wife scolded him constantly, and laid on his shoulders all the mischief that was done about the place; and the shuffler gave him half his own work to do, and hunted him about from dawn till past sunset. He was always going at the end of every week, but never gone; perhaps he had undergone too much in his wanderings, to be ready to begin them again; or perhaps either Cæsar or Harold, one or both, kept him at Friarswood. And there might be another reason, too, for no one had ever spoken to him like Mr. Cope. Very few had ever thrown him a kindly word, or seemed to treat him like a thing with feelings, and those few had been rough and unmannerly; but Mr. Cope's good-natured smile and pleasant manner had been a very different thing; and perhaps Paul promised to come to the Confirmation class, chiefly because of the friendly tone in which he was invited.

When there, he really liked it. He had always liked what he was taught, apart from the manner of teaching; and now both manner and lessons were delightful to him. His answers were admirable, and it was not all head knowledge, for very little more than a really kind way of putting it was needed, to make him turn in his loneliness to rest in the thought of the ever-present Father. Hard as the discipline of his workhouse home had been, it had kept him from much outward harm; the little he had seen in his wanderings had shocked him, and he was more untaught in evil than many lads who thought themselves more respectable, so there was no habit of wickedness to harden and blunt him; and the application of all he had learnt before, found his heart ready.

He had not gone to church since he left the workhouse: he did not think it belonged to vagabonds like him; besides, he always felt walls like a prison; and he had not profited much by the workhouse prayers, which were read on week-days by the master, and on Sundays by a chaplain, who always had more to do than he could manage, and only went to the paupers when they were very ill. But when Mr. Cope talked to him of the duty of going to church, he said, 'I will, Sir;' and he sat in the gallery with the young lads, who were not quite as delicate as Alfred.

The service seemed to rest him, and to be like being brought near a friend; and he had been told that church might always be his home. He took a pleasure in going thither—the more, perhaps, that he rather liked to shew how little he cared for remarks upon his appearance. There was a great deal of independence about him; and, having escaped from the unloving maintenance of the parish, while he had as yet been untaught what affection or gratitude meant, he *would* not be beholden to any one.

Scanty as were his wages, he would accept nothing from anybody; he daily bought his portion of bread from Mrs. King, but it was of no use for her to add a bit of cheese or bacon to it; he never would see the relish, and left it behind; and so he never would accept Mr. Cope's kind offers of giving him a bit of supper in his kitchen, perhaps because he was afraid of being said to go to the Rectory for the sake of what he could get.

He did not object to the farmer's beer, which was sometimes given him when any unusual extra work had been put on him. That was his right, for in truth the farmer did not pay him the value of his labour, and perhaps disliked him the more, because of knowing in his conscience that this was shameful extortion.

However, just at harvest time, when Paul's shoes had become very like what may be sometimes picked up by the roadside, Mr. Shepherd did actually bestow on him a pair that did not fit himself! Harold came home quite proud of them.

However, on the third day they were gone, and the farmer's voice was heard on the bridge, rating Paul violently for having changed them away for drink.

Mrs. King felt sorrowful; but, as Ellen said, 'What could you expect of him?' In spite of the affront, there was a sort of acquaintance now over the counter between Mrs. King and young Blackthorn; and when he came for his bread, she could not help saying, 'I'm sorry to see you in those again.'

'Why, the others hurt me so, I could hardly get about,' said Paul.

'Ah! poor lad, I suppose your feet has got spread with wearing those old ones; but you should try to use yourself to decent ones, or you'll soon be barefoot; and I do think it was a pity to drink them up.'

'That's all the farmer, Ma'am. He thinks one can't do anything but drink.'

'Well, what is become of them?'

'Why, you see, Ma'am, they just suited Dick Royston, and he wanted a pair of shoes, and I wanted a Bible and Prayer-book, so we changed 'em.'

When Ellen heard this, she could not help owning that Paul was a good boy after all, though it was in an odd sort of way. But, alas! when next he was to go to Mr. Cope, there was a hue-and-cry all over the hay-loft for the Prayer-book. There was no place to put it safely, or if there had been, Poor Paul was too great a sloven to think of any such thing; and as it was in a somewhat rubbishy state to begin with, it was most likely that one of the cows had eaten it with her hay; and all that could be said was, that it would have been worse if it had been the Bible.

As to Dick Royston, to find that he would change away his Bible for a pair of shoes, made Mrs. King doubly concerned that he should be a good deal thrown in Harold's way. There are many people who neglect their Bibles, and do not read them; but this may be from thoughtlessness or press of care, and is not like the wilful breaking with good, that it is to part with the Holy Scripture, save under the most dire necessity; and Dick was far from being in real want, nor was he ignorant, like Mr. Cope's poor Jem, for he had been to school, and could read well; but he was one of those many lads, who, alas! are everywhere to be found, who break loose from all restraint as soon as they can maintain themselves. They do their work pretty well, and are tolerably honest; but for the rest—alas! they seem to live without God. Prayers and Church they have left behind, as belonging to school-days; and in all their strength and health, their days of toil, their evenings of rude diversion, their Sundays of morning sleep, noonday basking in the sun, evening cricket, they have little more notion of anything concerning their souls than the horses they drive. If ever a fear comes over them, it seems a long long way off, a whole life-time before them; they are awkward, and in dread of one another's jeers and remarks; and if they ever wish to be better, they cast it from them by fancying that time must steady them when they have had their bit of fun, or that something will come from somewhere to change them all at once, and make it easy to them to be good—as if they were not making it harder each moment.

This sort of lad had been utterly let alone till Mr. Cope came; and Lady Jane and the school-master felt it was dreary work to train up nice lads in the school, only to see them run riot, and forget all good as soon as they thought themselves their own masters.

Mr. Cope was anxious to do the best he could for them, and the Confirmation made a good opportunity; but the boys did not like to be interfered with—it made them shy to be spoken to; and they liked lounging about much better than having to poke into that mind of theirs, which they carried somewhere about them, but did not like to stir up. They had no notion of going to school again—which no one wanted them to do—nor to church, because it was like little boys; and they wouldn't be obliged.

So Mr. Cope made little way with them; a few who had better parents came regularly to him, but others went off when they found it too much trouble, and behaved worse than ever by way of shewing they did not care. This folly had in some degree taken possession of Harold; and though he could not be as bad as were some of the others, he was fast growing impatient of restraint, and worried and angry, as if any word of good advice affronted him. Driven from home by the fear of disturbing Alfred, he was left the more to the company of boys who made him ashamed of being ordered by his mother; and there was a jaunty careless style about all his ways of talking and moving, that shewed there was something wrong about him—he scorned Ellen, and was as saucy as he dared even to his mother; and though Mr. Cope found him better instructed than most of his scholars, he saw him quite as idle, as restless at church, and as ready to whisper and grin at improper times, as many who had never been trained like him.

One August Sunday afternoon, Mrs. King was with Alfred while Ellen was at church. He was lying on his couch, very uncomfortable and fretful, when to the surprise of both, a knock was heard at the door. Mrs. King looked out of the window, and a smart, hard-looking, pigeon's-neck silk bonnet at once nodded to her, and a voice said, 'I've come over to see you, Cousin King, if you'll come down and let me in. I knew I should find you at home.'

'Betsey Hardman!' exclaimed Alfred, in dismay; 'you won't let her come up here, Mother?'

'Not if I can help it,' said Mrs. King, sighing. If there were a thing she disliked above all others, it was Sunday visiting.

'You must help it, Mother,' said Alfred, in his most pettish tones. 'I won't have her here, worrying with her voice like a hen cackling. Say you won't let her come her!'

'Very well,' said Mrs. King, in doubt of her own powers, and in haste to be decently civil.

'Say you won't,' repeated Alfred. 'Gadding about of a Sunday, and leaving her old sick mother—more shame for her! Promise, Mother!'

He had nearly begun to cry at his mother's unkindness in running down-stairs without making the promise, for, in fact, Mrs. King had too much conscience to gain present quiet for any one by promises she might be forced to break; and Betsey Hardman was only too well known.

Her mother was an aunt of Alfred's father, an old decrepit widow, nearly bed-ridden, but pretty well to do, by being maintained chiefly by her daughter, who made a good thing of taking in washing in the suburbs of Elbury, and always had a girl or two under her. She had neither had the education, nor the good training in service, that had fallen to Mrs. King's lot; and her way of life did not lead to softening her tongue or temper. Ellen called her vulgar, and though that is not a nice word to use, she was coarse in her ways of talking and thinking, loud-voiced, and unmannerly, although meaning to be very good-natured.

Alfred lay in fear of her step, ten times harder than Harold's in his most boisterous mood, coming clamp clamp! up the stairs; and her shrill voice— the same tone in which she bawled to her deaf mother, and hallooed to her girls when they were hanging out the clothes in the high wind—coming pitying him—ay, and perhaps her whole weight lumbering down on the couch beside him, shaking every joint in his body! His mother's ways, learnt in the Selby nursery, had made him more tender, and more easily fretted by such things, than most cottage lads, who would have been used to them, and never have thought of not liking to have every neighbour who chose running up into the room, and talking without regard to subject or tone.

He listened in a fright to the latch of the door, and the coming in. Betsey's voice came up, through every chink of the boards, whatever she did herself; and he could hear every word of her greeting, as she said how it was such a fine day, she said to Mother she would take a holiday, and come and see Cousin King and the poor lad: it must be mighty dull for him, moped up there.

Stump! stump! Was she coming? His mother was answering something too soft for him to hear.

'What, is he asleep?'

'O Mother, must you speak the truth?'

'Bless me! I should have thought a little cheerful company was good for him. Do you leave him quite alone? Well—' and there was a frightful noise of the foot of the heaviest chair on the floor. 'I'll sit down and wait a bit! Is he so very fractious, then?'

What was his mother saying? Alfred clenched his fist, and grinned anger at Betsey with closed teeth. There was the tiresome old word, 'Low—ay, so's my mother; but you should rise his spirits with company, you see; that's why I came over; as soon as ever I heard that there wasn't no hope of him, says I to Mother—'

What? What was that she had heard? There was his mother, probably trying to restrain her voice, for it came up now just loud enough to make it most distressing to try to catch the words, which sounded like something pitying. 'Ay, ay—just like his poor father; when they be decliny, it will come out one ways or another; and says I to Mother, I'll go over and cheer poor Cousin King up a bit, for you see, after all, if he'd lived, he'd be nothing but a burden, crippled up like that; and a lingering job is always bad for poor folks.'

Alfred leant upon his elbow, his eyes full stretched, but feeling as if all his senses had gone into his ears, in his agony to hear more; and he even seemed to catch his mother's voice, but there was no hope in that; it was of her knowing it would be all for the best; and the sadness of it told him that she believed the same as Betsey. Then came, 'Yes; I declare it gave me such a turn, you might have knocked me down with a feather. I asked Mr. Blunt to come in and see what's good for Mother, she feels so weak at times, and has such a noise in her head, just like the regiment playing drums, she says, till she can't hardly bear herself; and so what do you think he says? Don't wrap up her head so warm, says he—a pretty thing for a doctor to say, as if a poor old creature like that, past seventy years old, could go without a bit of flannel to her head, and her three night-caps, and a shawl over them when there's a draught. I say, Cousin, I ha'n't got much opinion of Mr. Blunt. Why don't you get some of them boxes of pills, that does cures wonderful? Ever so many lords and ladies cured of a perplexity fit, by only just taking an imposing draught or two.'

Another time Alfred would have laughed at the very imposing draught, that was said to cure lords and ladies of this jumble between apoplexy and paralysis; but this was no moment for laughing, and he was in despair at fancying his mother wanted to lead her off on the quack medicine; but she went on.

'Well, only read the papers that come with them. I make my girl Sally read 'em all to me, being that she's a better scholar; and the long words is quite heavenly—I declare there ain't one of them shorter than peregrination. I'd have brought one of them over to shew you if I hadn't come away in a hurry, because Evans's cart was going out to the merry orchard, and says I to Mother, Well, I'll get a lift now there's such a chance to Friarswood: it'll do them all a bit of good to see a bit of cheerful company, seeing, as Mr. Blunt says, that poor lad is going after his father as fast as can be. Dear me, says I, you don't say so, such a fine healthy-looking chap as he was. Yes, he says, but it's in the constitution; it's getting to the lungs, and he'll never last out the winter.'

Alfred listened for the tone of his mother's voice; he knew he should judge by that, even without catching the words—low, subdued, sad—he almost thought she began with 'Yes.'

All the rest that he heard passed by him merely as a sound, noted no more than the lowing of the cattle, or the drone of the thrashing machine. He lay half lifted up on his pillows, drawing his breath short with apprehension; his days were numbered, and death was coming fast, fast, straight upon him. He felt it within himself—he knew now the meaning of the pain and sinking, the shortness of breath and choking of throat that had been growing on him through the long summer days; he was being 'cut off with pining sickness,' and his sentence had gone forth. He would have screamed for his mother in the sore terror and agony that had come over him, in hopes she might drive the notion from him; but the dread of seeing her followed by that woman kept his lips shut, except for his long gasps of breath.

And she could not keep him—Mr. Blunt could not keep him; no one could stay the hand that had touched him! Prayer! They had prayed for his father, for Charlie, but it had not been God's Will. He had himself many times prayed to recover, and it had not been granted—he was worse and worse.

Moreover, whither did that path of suffering lead? Up rose before Alfred the thought of living after the unknown passage, and of answering for all he had done; and now the faults he had refused to call to mind when he was told of chastisement, came and stood up of themselves. Bred up to know the good, he had not loved it; he had cared for his own pleasure, not for God; he had not heeded the comfort of his widowed mother; he had been careless of the honour of God's House, said and heard prayers without minding them; he had been disrespectful and ill-behaved at my Lady's—he had been bad in every way; and when illness came, how rebellious and murmuring he had been, how unkind he had been to his patient mother, sister, and brother; and when Mr. Cope had told him it was meant to lead him to repent, he would not hear; and now it was too late, the door would be shut. He had always heard that there was a time when sorrow was no use, when the offer of being saved had been thrown away.

When Ellen came in, and after a short greeting to Betsey Hardman, went up-stairs, she found Alfred lying back on his pillow, deadly white, the beads of dew standing on his brow, and his breath in gasps. She would have shrieked for her mother, but he held out his hand, and said, in a low hoarse whisper, 'Ellen, is it true?'

'What, Alfy dear? What is the matter?'

'What *she* says.'

'Who? Betsey Hardman? Dear dear Alf, is it anything dreadful?'

'That I shall die,' said Alfred, his eyes growing round with terror again. 'That Mr. Blunt said I couldn't last out the winter.'

'Dear Alfy, don't!' cried Ellen, throwing her arms round him, and kissing him with all her might; 'don't fancy it! She's always gossiping and gadding about, and don't know what she says, and she'd got no business to tell stories to frighten my darling!' she exclaimed, sobbing with agitation. 'I'm sure Mr. Blunt never said no such thing!'

'But Mother thinks it, Ellen.'

'She doesn't, she can't!' cried Ellen vehemently; 'I know she doesn't, or she could never go about as she does. I'll call her up and ask her, to satisfy you.'

'No, no, not while that woman is there!' cried Alfred, holding her by the dress; 'I'll not have *her* coming up.'

Even while he spoke, however, Mrs. King was coming. Betsey had spied an old acquaintance on the way from church, and had popped out to speak to her, and Mrs. King caught that moment for coming up. She understood all, for she had been sitting in great distress, lest Alfred should be listening to every word which she was unable to silence, and about which Betsey was quite thoughtless. So many people of her degree would talk to the patient about himself and his danger, and go on constantly before him with all their fears, and the doctor's opinions, that Betsey had never thought of there being more consideration and tenderness shewn in this house, nor that Mrs. King would have hidden any pressing danger from the sick person; but such plain words had not yet passed between her and Mr. Blunt; and though she had long felt what Alfred's illness would come to, the perception had rather grown on her than come at any particular moment.

Now when Ellen, with tears and agitation, asked what that Betsey had been saying to frighten Alfred so, and when she saw her poor boy's look at her, and heard his sob, 'Oh, Mother!' it was almost too much for her, and she went up and kissed him, and laid him down less uneasily, but he felt a great tear fall on his face.

'It's not true, Mother, I'm sure it is not true,' cried Ellen; 'she ought—'

Mrs. King looked at her daughter with a sad sweet face, that stopped her short, and brought the sense over her too. 'Did he say so, Mother?' said Alfred.

'Not to me, dear,' she answered; 'but, Ellen, she's coming back! She'll be up here if you don't go down.'

Poor Ellen! what would she not have given for power to listen to her mother, and cry at her ease? But she was forced to hurry, or Betsey would have been half-way up-stairs in another instant. She was a hopeful girl, however, and after that 'not to me,' resolved to believe nothing of the matter. Mrs. King knelt down by her son, and looked at him tenderly; and then, as his eyes went on begging for an answer, she said, 'Dr. Blunt never told me there was no hope, my dear, and everything lies in God's power.'

'But you don't think I shall get well, Mother?'

'I don't feel as if you would, my boy,' she said, very low, and fondling him all the time. 'You've got to cough like Father and Charlie, and—though He might raise my boy up—yet anyhow, Alfy boy, if God sees it good for us, it *will* be good for us, and we shall be helped through with it.'

'But I'm not good, Mother! What will become of me?'

'Perhaps the hearing this is all out of God's mercy, to give you time to get ready, my dear. You are no worse now than you were this morning; you are not like to go yet awhile. No, indeed, my child; so if you don't put off any longer—'

'Mother!' called up Ellen. She was in despair. Betsey was not to be kept by her from satisfying herself upon Alfred's looks, and Mrs. King was only in time to meet her on the stairs, and tell her that he was so weak and low, that he could not be seen now, she could not tell how it would be when he had had his tea.

Ellen thought she had never had so distressing a tea-drinking in her life, as the being obliged to sit listening civilly to Betsey's long story about the trouble she had about a stocking of Mrs. Martin's that was lost in the wash, and that had gone to Miss Rosa Marlowe, because Mrs. Martin had her things marked with a badly-done K. E. M., and all that Mrs. Martin's Maria and all Miss Marlowe's Jane had said about it, and all Betsey's 'Says I to Mother,'—when she was so longing to be watching poor Alfred, and how her mother could sit so quietly making tea, and answering so civilly, she could not guess; but Mrs. King had that sense of propriety and desire to do as she would be done by, which is the very substance of Christian courtesy, the very want of which made Betsey, with all her wish to be kind, a real oppression and burthen to the whole party.

And where was Harold? Ellen had not seen him coming out of church, but meal-times were pretty certain to bring him home.

'Oh,' said Betsey, 'I'll warrant he is off to the merry orchard.'

'I hope not,' said Mrs. King gravely.

'He never would,' said Ellen, in anger.

'Ah, well, I always said I didn't see no harm in a lad getting a bit of pleasure.'

'No, indeed,' said Mrs. King. 'Harold knows I would not stint him in the fruit nor in the pleasure, but I should be much vexed if he could go out on a Sunday, buying and selling, among such a lot as meet at that orchard.'

'Well, I'm sure I don't know when poor folks is to have a holiday if not on a Sunday, and the poor boy must be terrible moped with his brother so ill.'

'Not doing thine own pleasure on My holy day,' thought Ellen, but she did not say it, for her mother could not bear for texts to be quoted at people. But her heart was very heavy; and when she went up with some tea to Alfred, she looked from the window to see whether, as she hoped, Harold might be in Paul's hay-loft, preferring going without his tea to being teased by Betsey. Paul sat in his loft, with his Bible on his knee, and his head on Cæsar's neck.

'Alfred,' said Ellen, 'do you know where Harold is? Sure he is not gone to the merry orchard?'

'Is not he come home?' said Alfred. 'Oh, then he is! He is gone to the merry orchard, breaking Sunday with Dick Royston! And by-and-by he'll be ill, and die, and be as miserable as I am!' And Alfred cried as Ellen had never seen him cry.

CHAPTER VI—THE MERRY ORCHARD

Where was Harold?

Still the evening went on, and he did not come. Alfred had worn himself out with his fit of crying, and lay quite still, either asleep, or looking so like it, that when Betsey had finished her tea, and again began asking to see him, Ellen could honestly declare that he was asleep.

Betsey had bidden them good-bye, more than half affronted at not being able to report to her mother all about his looks, though she carried with her a basket of gooseberries and French beans, and Mrs. King walked all the way down the lane with her, and tried to shew an interest in all she said, to make up for the disappointment.

Maybe likewise Mrs. King felt it a relief to her uneasiness to look up and down the road, and along the river, and into the farm-yard, in the hope that Harold might be in sight; but nothing was to be seen on the road, but Master Norland, his wife, and baby, soberly taking their Sunday walk; nor by the river, except the ducks, who seemed to be enjoying their evening bath, and almost asleep on the water; nor in the yard, except Paul Blackthorn, who had come down from his perch to drive the horses in from the home-field, and shut the stable up for the night.

She could not help stopping a moment at the gate, and calling out to Paul to ask whether he had seen anything of Harold. He seemed to have a great mind not to hear, and turned very slowly with his shoulder towards her, making a sound like 'Eh?' as if to ask what she said.

'Have you seen my boy Harold?'

'I saw him in the morning.'

'Have you not seen him since? Didn't he go to church with you?'

'No; I don't go to Sunday school.'

'Was he there?'

She did not receive any answer.

'Do you know if many of the boys are gone to the merry orchard?'

'Ay.'

'Well, you are a good lad not to be one of them.'

'Hadn't got any money,' said Paul gruffly; but Mrs. King thought he said so chiefly from dislike to be praised, and that there had been some principle as well as poverty to keep him away.

'It might be better if no one had it on a Sunday,' she could not help sighing out as she looked anxiously along the lane ere turning in, and then said, 'My good lad, I don't want to get you to be telling tales, but it would set my heart at rest, and his poor brother's up there, if you could tell me he is not gone to Briar Alley.'

Paul turned up his face from the gate upon which he was leaning his elbows, and gazed for a moment at her sad, meek, anxious face, then exclaimed, 'I can't think how he could!'

Poor Paul! was it not crossing him how impossible it would seem to do anything to vex one who so cared for him?

'Then he is gone,' she said mournfully.

'They were all at him,' said Paul; 'and he said he'd never seen what it was like. Please don't take on, Missus; he's right kind and good-hearted, and wanted to treat me.'

'I had rather he had hearkened to you, my boy,' said Mrs. King.

'I don't know why he should do that,' said Paul, perhaps meaning that a boy who heeded not such a mother would certainly heed no one else. 'But please, Missus,' he added, 'don't beat him, for you made me tell on him.'

'Beat him! no,' said Mrs. King, with a sad smile; 'he's too big a boy for me to manage that way. I can't do more than grieve if he lets himself be led away.'

'Then I'd like to beat him myself if he grieves you!' burst out Paul, doubling up his brown fist with indignation.

'But you won't,' said Mrs. King gently; 'I don't want to make a quarrel among you, and I hope you'll help to keep him out of bad ways, Paul. I look to you for it. Good-night.'

Perhaps the darkness and her own warm feeling made her forget the condition of that hand; at any rate, as she said Good-night she took it in her own and shook it heartily, and then she went in.

Paul did not say Good-night in answer; but when she had turned away, his head went down between his two crossed arms upon the top of the gate, and he did not move for many many minutes, except that his shoulders shook and shook again, for he was sobbing as he had never sobbed since Granny Moll died. If home and home love were not matters of course to you, you might guess what strange new fountains of feeling were stirred in the wild but not untaught boy, by that face, that voice, that touch.

And Mrs. King, as she walked to her own door in the twilight, with bitter pain in her heart, could not help thinking of those from the highways and hedges who flocked to the feast set at naught by such as were bidden.

A sad and mournful Sunday evening was that to the mother and daughter, as each sat over her Bible. Mrs. King would not talk to Ellen, for fear of awakening Alfred; not that low voices would have done so, but Ellen was already much upset by what she had heard and seen, and to talk it over would have brought on a fit of violent crying; so her mother thought it safest to say nothing. They would have read their Bible to one another, but each had her voice so choked with tears, that it would not do.

That Alfred was sinking away into the grave, was no news to Mrs. King; but perhaps it had never been so plainly spoken to her before, and his own knowledge of it seemed to make it more sure; but broken-hearted as she felt, she had been learning to submit to this, and it might be better and safer for him, she thought, to be aware of his state, and more ready to do his best with the time left to him. That was not the freshest sorrow, or more truly a darker cloud had come over, namely, the feeling, so terrible to a good careful mother, that her son is breaking out of the courses to which she has endeavoured and prayed to bring him up—that he is casting off restraint, and running into evil that may be the beginning of ruin, and with no father's hand to hold him in.

O Harold, had you but seen the thick tears dropping on the walnut table behind the arm that hid her face from Ellen, you would not have thought your fun worth them!

That merry orchard was about three miles from Friarswood. It belonged to a man who kept a small public-house, and had a little farm, and a large garden, with several cherry trees, which in May were perfect gardens of blossoms, white as snow, and in August with small black fruit of the sort known as merries; and unhappily the fertile produce of these trees became a great temptation to the owner and to all the villagers around.

As Sunday was the only day when people could be at leisure, he chose three Sundays when the cherries were ripe for throwing open his orchard to all who chose to come and buy and eat the fruit, and of course cakes and drink of various kinds were also sold. It was a solitary spot, out of the way of the police, or the selling in church-time would have been stopped; but as there may be cases of real distress, the law does not shut up all houses for selling food and drink on a Sunday, so others, where there is no necessity, take advantage of it; and so for miles round all the idle young people and children would call it a holiday to go away from their churches to eat cherries at Briar

Alley, buying and selling on a Sunday, noisy and clamorous, and forgetting utterly that it was the Lord's Day, not their day of idle pleasure.

It was a sad pity that an innocent feast of fruit should be almost out of reach, unless enjoyed in this manner. To be sure, merries might be bought any day of the week at Briar Alley, and were hawked up and down Friarswood so cheaply that any one might get a mouth as purple as the black spaniel's any day in the season; but that was nothing to the fun of going with numbers, and numbers never could go except on a Sunday. But if people wish to serve God truly, why, they must make up their minds to miss pleasures for His sake, and this was one to begin with; and I am much mistaken if the happiness of the week would not have turned out greater in the end with him. Ay, and as to the owner of the trees, who said he was a poor man, and could not afford to lose the profit, I believe that if he would have trusted God and kept His commandment, his profit in the long run would have been greater here, to say nothing of the peril to his own soul of doing wrong, and leading so many into temptation.

The Kings had been bred up to think a Sunday going to the merry orchard a thing never to be done; and in his most idle days Alfred would never have dreamt of such a thing. Indeed, their good mother always managed to have some treat to make up for it when they were little; and they certainly never wanted for merries, nay, a merry pudding had been their dinner this very day, with savage-looking purple juice and scalding hot stones. If Harold went it was for the frolic, not for want of the dainty; and wrong as it was, his mother was grieving more at the thought of his casting away the restraint of his old habits than for the one action. One son going away into the unseen world, the other being led away from the paths of right—no wonder she wept as she tried to read!

At last voices were coming, and very loud ones. The summer night was so still, they could be heard a great way—those rude coarse voices of village boys boasting and jeering one another.

'I say, wouldn't you like to be one of they chaps at Ragglesford School?'

'What lots they bought there on Saturday, to be sure!'

'Well they may: they've lots of tin!'

'Have they? How d'ye know?'

'Why, the money-letters! Don't I know the feel of them—directed to master this and master that, and with a seal and a card, and half a sovereign, or maybe a whole one, under it; and such lots as they gets before the holidays—that's to go home, you see.'

'Well, it's a shame such little impudent rogues should get so much without ever doing a stroke of work for it.'

'I say, Harold, don't ye never put one of they letters in your pocket?'

'For shame, Dick!'

'Ha! I shall know where to come when I wants half a sovereign or so!'

'No, you won't.'

It was only these last two or three speeches that reached the cottage at all clearly; and they were followed by a sound as if Harold had fallen upon one of the others, and they were holding him off, with halloos and shouts of hoarse laughing, which broke Alfred's sleep, and his voice came down-stairs with a startled cry of 'Mother! Mother! what is that?' She ran up-stairs in haste, and Ellen threw the door open. The sudden display of the light silenced the noisy boys; and Harold came slowly up the garden-path, pretty certain of a scolding, and prepared to feel it as little as he could help.

'Well, Master, a nice sort of a way of spending a Sunday evening this!' began Ellen; 'and coming hollaing up the lane, just on purpose to wake poor Alfred, when he's so ill!'

'I'm sure I never meant to wake him.'

'Then what did you bring all that good-for-nothing set roaring and shouting up the road for? And just this evening, too, when one would have thought you would we have cared for poor Mother and Alfred,' said she, crying.

'Why, what's the matter now?' said Harold.

'Oh, they've been saying he can't live out the winter,' said Ellen, shedding the tears that had been kept back all this time, and broke out now with double force, in her grief for one brother and vexation with the other.

But next winter seemed a great way off to Harold, and he was put out besides, so he did not seem shocked, especially as he was reproached with not feeling what he did not know; so all he did was to say angrily, 'And how was I to know that?'

'Of course you don't know anything, going scampering over the country with the worst lot you can find, away from church and all, not caring for anything! Poor Mother! she never thought one of her lads would come to that!'

'Plenty does so, without never such a fuss,' said Harold. 'Why, what harm is there in eating a few cherries?'

There would be very little pleasure or use in knowing what a wrangling went on all the time Mrs. King was up-stairs putting Alfred to bed. Ellen had all the right on her side, but she did not use it wisely; she was very unhappy, and much displeased with Harold, and so she had it all out in a fretful manner that made him more cross and less feeling than was his nature.

There was something he did feel, however—and that was his mother's pale, worn, sorrowful face, when she came down-stairs and hushed Ellen, but did not speak to him. They took down the books, read their chapter, and she read prayers very low, and not quite steadily. He would have liked very much to have told her he felt sorry, but he was too proud to do so after having shewn Ellen he was above caring for such nonsense.

So they all went to bed, Harold on a little landing at the top of the stairs; but —whether it was from the pounds of merry-stones he had swallowed, or the talk he had had with his sister—he could not go to sleep, and lay tossing and tumbling about, thinking it very odd he had not heeded more what Ellen had said when he first came in, and the notion dawning on him more and more, that day after day would come and make Alfred worse, and that by the time summer came again he should be alone. Who could have said it? Why had not he asked? What could he have been thinking about? It should not be true! A sort of frenzy to speak to some one, and hear the real meaning of those words, so as to make sure they were only Ellen's nonsense, came over him in the silent darkness. Presently he heard Alfred moving on his pillow, for the door was open for the heat; and that long long sigh made him call in a whisper, 'Alf, are you awake?'

In another moment Harold was by his brother's side. 'Alf! Alf! are you worse?' he asked, whispering.

'No.'

'Then what's all this? What did they say? It's all stuff; I'm sure it is, and you're getting better. But what did Ellen mean?'

'No, Harold,' said Alfred, getting his brother's hand in his, 'it's not stuff; I shan't get well; I'm going after poor Charlie; and don't you be a bad lad,

Harold, and run away from your church, for you don't know—how bad it feels to—' and Alfred turned his face down, for the tears were coming thick.

'But you aren't going to die, Alf. Charlie never was like you, I know he wasn't; he was always coughing. It is all Ellen. Who said it? I won't let them.'

'The doctor said it to Betsey Hardman,' said Alfred; and his cough was only too like his brother's.

Harold would have said a great deal in contempt of Betsey Hardman, but Alfred did not let him.

'You'll wake Mother,' he said. 'Hush, Harold, don't go stamping about; I can't bear it! No, I don't want any one to tell me now; I've been getting worse ever since I was taken, and—oh! be quiet, Harold.'

'I can't be quiet,' sobbed Harold, coming nearer to him. 'O Alf! I can't spare you! There hasn't been no proper downright fun without you, and—'

Harold had lain down by him and clung to his hand, trying not to sob aloud.

'O Harold!' sighed Alfred, 'I don't think I should mind—at least not so much —if I hadn't been such a bad boy.'

'You, Alfy! Who was ever a good boy if you was not?'

'Hush! You forget all about when I was up at my Lady's, and all that. Oh! and how bad I behaved at church, and when I was so saucy to Master about the marbles; and so often I've not minded Mother. O Harold! and God judges one for everything!'

What a sad terrified voice it was!

'Oh! don't go on so, Alf! I can't bear it! Why, we are but boys; and those things were so long ago! God will not be hard on little boys. He is merciful, don't you know?'

'But when I knew it was wrong, I did the worst I could!' said Alfred. 'Oh, if I could only begin all over again, now I do care! Only, Harold, Harold, you are well; you can be good now when there's time.'

'I'll be ever so good if you'll only get well,' said Harold. 'I wouldn't have gone to that there place to-night; but 'tis so terribly dull, and one must do something.'

'But in church-time, and on Sunday!'

'Well, I'll never do it again; but it was so sunshiny, and they were all making such fun, you see, and it did seem so stuffy, and so long and tiresome, I couldn't help it, you see.'

Alfred did not think of asking how, if Harold could not help it this time, he could be sure of never doing so again. He was more inclined to dwell on himself, and went back to that one sentence, 'God judges us for everything.' Harold thought he meant it for him, and exclaimed,

'Yes, yes, I know, but—oh, Alf, you shouldn't frighten one so; I never meant no harm.'

'I wasn't thinking about that,' sighed Alfred. 'I was wishing I'd been a better lad; but I've been worse, and crosser, and more unkind, ever since I was ill. O Harold! what shall I do?'

'Don't go on that way,' said Harold, crying bitterly. 'Say your prayers, and maybe you will get well; and then in the morning I'll ask Mr. Cope to come down, and he'll tell you not to mind.'

'I wouldn't listen to Mr. Cope when he told me to be sorry for my sins; and oh, Harold, if we are not sorry, you know they will not be taken away.'

'Well, but you are sorry now.'

'I have heard tell that there are two ways of being sorry, and I don't know if mine is the right.'

'I tell you I'll fetch Mr. Cope in the morning; and when the doctor comes he'll be sure to say it is all a pack of stuff, and you need not be fretting yourself.'

When Harold awoke in the morning, he found himself lying wrapped in his coverlet on Alfred's bed, and then he remembered all about it, and looked in haste, as though he expected to see some sudden and terrible change in his brother.

But Alfred was looking cheerful, he had awakened without discomfort; and with some amusement, was watching the starts and movements, the grunts and groans, of Harold's waking. The morning air and the ordinary look of things, had driven away the gloomy thoughts of evening, and he chiefly thought of them as something strange and dreadful, and yet not quite a dream.

'Don't tell Mother,' whispered Harold, recollecting himself, and starting up quietly.

'But you'll fetch Mr. Cope,' said Alfred earnestly.

Harold had begun not to like the notion of meeting Mr. Cope, lest he should hear something of yesterday's doings, and he did not like Alfred or himself to think of last night's alarm, so he said, 'Oh, very well, I'll see about it.'

He had not made up his mind. Very likely, if chance had brought him face to face with Mr. Cope, he would have spoken about Alfred as the best way to hinder the Curate from reproving himself; but he had not that right sort of boldness which would have made him go to meet the reproof he so richly deserved, and he was trying to persuade himself either that when Alfred was amused and cheery, he would forget all about 'that there Betsey's nonsense,' or else that Mr. Cope might come that way of himself.

But Alfred was not likely to forget. What he had heard hung on him through all the little occupations of the morning, and made him meek and gentle under them, and he was reckoning constantly upon Mr. Cope's coming, fastening on the notion as if he were able to save him.

Still the Curate came not, and Alfred became grieved, feeling as if he was neglected.

Mr. Blunt, however, came, and at any rate he would have it out with him; so he asked at once very straightforwardly, 'Am I going to die, Sir?'

'Why, what's put that in your head?' said the doctor.

'There was a person here talking last night, Sir,' said Mrs. King.

'Well, but am I?' said Alfred impatiently.

'Not just yet, I hope,' said Mr. Blunt cheerfully. 'You are weak, but you'll pick up again.'

'But of this?' persisted Alfred, who was not to be trifled with.

Mr. Blunt saw he must be in earnest.

'My boy,' he said, 'I'm afraid it is not a thing to be got over. I'll do the best I can for you, by God's blessing; and if you get through the winter, and it is a mild spring, you might do; but you'd better settle your mind that you can't be many years for this world.'

Many years! that sounded like a reprieve, and sent gladness into Ellen's heart; but somehow it did not seem in the same light to Alfred; he felt that if he were slowly going down hill and wasting away, so as to have no more health or strength in which to live differently from ever before, the length of time was not much to him, and in his sickly impatience he would almost have preferred that it should not be what Betsey kindly called 'a lingering job.'

There he lay after Mr. Blunt was gone, not giving Ellen any trouble, except by the sad thoughtfulness of his face, as he lay dwelling on all that he wanted to say to Mr. Cope, and the terror of his sin and of judgment sweeping over him every now and then.

Still Mr. Cope came not. Alfred at last began to wonder aloud, and asked if Harold had said anything about it when he came in to dinner; but he heard that Harold had only rushed in for a moment, snatched up a lump of bread and cheese, and made off to the river with some of the lads who meant to spend the noon-tide rest in bathing.

When he came for the evening letters he was caught, and Mr. Cope was asked for; and then it came out that Harold had never given the message at all.

Alfred, greatly hurt, and sadly worn by his day of expectation, had no self-restraint left, and flew out into a regular passion, calling his brother angry names. Harold, just as passionate, went into a rage too, and scolded his brother for his fancies. Mrs. King, in great displeasure, turned him out, and he rushed off to ride like one mad to Elbury; and poor Alfred remained so much shocked at his own outbreak, just when he meant to have been good ever after, and sobbing so miserably, that no one could calm him at all; and Ellen, as the only hope, put on her bonnet to fetch Mr. Cope.

At that moment Paul was come for his bit of bread. She found him looking dismayed at the sounds of violent weeping from above, and he asked what it was.

'Oh, Alfred is so low and so bad, and he wants Mr. Cope! Here's your bread, don't keep me!'

'Let me go! I'll be quicker!' cried Paul; and before she could thank him, he was down the garden and right across the first field.

Alfred had had time to cry himself exhausted, and to be lying very still, almost faint, before Mr. Cope came in in the summer twilight. Good Paul! He had found that Mr. Cope was dining at Ragglesford and had run all the way thither; and here was the kind young Curate, quite breathless with his haste, and never regretting the cheerful party whence he had been called away. All Alfred could say was, 'O Sir, I shall die; and I'm a bad boy, and wouldn't heed you when you said so.'

'And God has made you see your sins, my poor boy,' said Mr. Cope. 'That is a great blessing.'

'But if I can't do anything to make up for them, what's the use? And I never shall be well again.'

'You can't make up for them; but there is One Who has made up for them, if you will only truly repent.'

'I wasn't sorry till I knew I should die,' said Alfred.

'No, your sins did not come home to you! Now, do you know what they are?'

'Oh yes; I've been a bad boy to Mother, and at church; and I've been cross to Ellen, and quarrelled with Harold; and I was so audacious at my Lady's, they couldn't keep me. I never did want really to be good. Oh! I know I shall go to the bad place!'

'No, Alfred, not if you so repent, that you can hold to our Blessed Saviour's promise. There is a fountain open for sin and all uncleanness.'

'It is very good of Him,' said Alfred, a little more tranquilly, not in the half-sob in which he had before spoken.

'Most merciful!' said Mr. Cope.

'But does it mean me?' continued Alfred.

'You were baptized, Alfred, you have a right to all His promises of pardon.' And he repeated the blessed sentences:

'Come unto Me, all that travail and are heavy laden, and I will refresh you.'

'God so loved the world, that He gave His only-begotten Son, to the end that all that believe in Him should not perish, but have everlasting life.'

'But how ought I to believe, Sir?'

'You say you feel what your sins are; think of them all as you lie, each one as you remember it; say it out in your heart to our Saviour, and pray God to forgive it for His sake, and then think that it cost some of the pain He bore on the Cross, some of the drops of His agony in the Garden. Each sin of ours was indeed of that burden!'

'Oh, that will make them seem so bad!'

'Indeed it does; but how it will make you love Him, and feel thankful to Him, and anxious not to waste the sufferings borne for your sake, and glad, perhaps, that you are bearing some small thing yourself. But you are spent, and I had better not talk more now. Let me read you a few prayers to help you, and then I will leave you, and come again to-morrow.'

How differently those Prayers and Psalms sounded to Alfred now that he had really a heart grieved and wearied with the burthen of sin! The point was to make his not a frightened heart, but a contrite heart.

CHAPTER VII—HAROLD TAKES A WRONG TURN

Mrs. King was very anxious about Alfred for many hours after this visit from the Curate, for he was continually crying, not violently, but the tears flowing quietly from his eyes as he lay, thinking. Sometimes it was the badness of the faults as he saw them now, looking so very different from what they did when they were committed in the carelessness of fun and high spirits, or viewed afterwards in the hardening light of self-justification. Now they did look so wantonly hard and rude—unkind to his sister, ruinous to Harold, regardless of his widowed mother, reckless of his God—that each one seemed to cut into him with a sense of its own badness, and he was quite as much grieved as afraid; he hated the fault, and hated himself for it.

Indeed, he was growing less afraid, for the sorrow seemed to swallow that up; the grief at having offended One so loving was putting out the terror of being punished; or rather, when he thought that this illness was punishment, he was almost glad to have some of what he deserved; just as when he was a little boy, he really used to be happier afterwards for having been whipped and put in the corner, because that was like making it up. Though he knew very well that if he had ten thousand times worse than this to bear, it would not be making up for his faults, and he felt now that one of them had been his 'despising the chastening of the Lord.' And then the thought of what had made up for it would come: and though he had known of it all his life, and heeded it all too little, now that his heart was tender, and he had felt some of the horror and pain of sin, he took it all home now, and clung to it. He recollected the verses about that One kneeling—nay, falling on the ground, in the cold dewy night, with the chosen friends who could not watch with Him, and the agony and misery that every one in all the world deserved to feel, gathering on Him, Who had done no wrong, and making His brow stream with great drops of Blood.

And the tortures, the shame, the slow Death—circumstance after circumstance came to his mind, and 'for me,' 'this fault of mine helped,' would rise with it, and the tears trickled down at the thought of the suffering and of the Love that had caused it to be undergone.

Once he raised up his head, and saw through the window the deep dark-blue sky, and the stars, twinkling and sparkling away; that pale band of light, the Milky Way, which they say is made of countless stars too far off to be distinguished, and looking like a cloud, and on it the larger, brighter burnished stars, differing from one another in glory. He thought of some lines in a book Miss Jane once gave Ellen, which said of the stars:

'The Lord resigned them all to gain
The bliss of pardoning thee.'

And when he thought that it was the King of those stars Who was scourged and spit on, and for the sake of *his* faults, the loving tears came again, and he turned to another hymn of Ellen's:

'Rock of Ages, cleft for me,
Let me hide myself in Thee!'

And going on with this, he fell into a more quiet sleep than he had had for many nights.

Alfred had worked up his mind to a point where it could not long remain; and when he awoke in the morning, the common affairs of the day occupied him in a way that was not hurtful to him, as the one chief thought was ever present, only laid away for a time, and helping him when he might have been fretful or impatient.

He was anxious for Mr. Cope, and grateful when he saw him coming early in the day. Mr. Cope did not, however, say anything very new. He chiefly wished to shew Alfred that he must not think all his struggle with sin over, and that he had nothing to do but to lie still and be pardoned. There was much more work, as he would find, when the present strong feeling should grow a little blunt; he would have to keep his will bent to bear what was sent by God, and to prove his repentance by curing himself of all his bad habits of peevishness and exacting; to learn, in fact, to take up his cross.

Alfred feebly promised to try, and it did not seem so difficult just then. The days were becoming cooler, and he did not feel quite so ill; and though he did not know how much this helped him, it made it much easier to act on his good resolutions. Miss Selby came to see him, and was quite delighted to see him looking so much less uncomfortable and dismal.

'Why, Alfred,' said she, 'you must be much better.'

Ellen looked mournful at this, and shook her head so that Miss Jane turned her bright face to her in alarm.

'No, Ma'am,' said Alfred. 'Dr. Blunt says I can never get over it.'

'And does that make you glad?' almost gasped Miss Jane.

'No, Ma'am,' said Alfred; 'but Mr. Cope has been talking to me, and made it all so—'

He could not get out the words; and, besides, he saw Miss Jane's eyes winking very fast to check the tears, and Ellen's had begun to rain down fast.

'I didn't mean to be silly,' said little Jane, in rather a trembling voice; 'but I'm sorry—no—I'm glad you are happy and good, Alfred.'

'Not good, Miss Jane,' cried Alfred; 'I'm such a bad boy, but there are such good things as I never minded before—'

'Well then, I think you'll like what I've brought you,' said Jane eagerly.

It was a little framed picture of our Blessed Lord on His Cross, all darkness round, and the Inscription above His Head; and Miss Jane had painted, in tall Old English red letters, under it the two words, 'For me.'

Alfred looked at it as if indeed it would be a great comfort to him to be always reminded by the eye, of how 'He was wounded for our transgressions, and bruised for our iniquities.'

He thanked Miss Jane with all his heart, and she and Ellen soon found a place to hang it up well in his sight. It was a pretty bright sight to see her insisting on holding the nail for it, and then playfully pretending to shrink and fancy that Ellen would hammer her fingers.

Alfred could enjoy the sunshine of his sick-room again; and Ellen and his mother down-stairs told Miss Selby, with many tears, of the happy change that had come over him ever since he had resigned himself to give up hopes of life. Mrs. King looked so peaceful and thankful, that little Jane could hardly understand what it was that made her so much more at rest.

Even Ellen, though her heart ached at the hope having gone out, and left a dark place where it had been, felt the great relief from hour to hour of not being fretted and snarled at for whatever she either did or left undone. Thanks and smiles were much pleasanter payment than groans, murmurs, and scoldings; and the brother and sister sometimes grew quite cheerful and merry together, as Alfred lay raised up to look over the hedge into the harvest-field across the meadow, where the reaper and his wife might be seen gathering the brown ears round, and cutting them with the sickle, and others going after to bind them into the glorious wheat sheaves that leant against each other in heaps of blessed promise of plenty.

Paul tried reaping; but the first thing he did was to make a terrible cut in his hand, which the shuffler told him was for good luck! Some of the women in the field bound it up, but he was good for nothing after it except going after the cattle, and so he was likely to lose all the chance of earning himself any better clothes in harvest-time.

Harold grumbled dreadfully that his mother could not spare him to go harvesting beyond their own tiny quarter of an acre of wheat. The post made it impossible for him to go out to work like the labourers; and besides, his mother did not think he had gained much good in hay-time, and wished to keep him from the boys.

Very hard he thought it; and to hear him grumble, any one would have thought Mrs. King was a tyrant far worse than Farmer Shepherd, working the flesh off his bones, taking away the fun and the payment alike.

The truth was, that the morning when Harold threw away from him the thought of his brother's danger, and broke all his promises to him in the selfish fear of a rebuke from the clergyman, had been one of the turning-points of his life, and a turning-point for the bad. It had been a hardening of his heart, just as it had begun to be touched, and a letting in of evil spirits instead of good ones.

He became more than ever afraid of Mr. Cope, and shirked going near him so as to be spoken to; he cut Ellen off short if she said a word to him, and avoided being with Alfred, partly because it made him melancholy, partly because he was afraid of Alfred's again talking to him about the evil of his ways. In reality, his secret soul was wretched at the thought of losing his brother; but he tried to put the notion away from him, and to drown it in the noisiest jokes and most riotous sports he could meet with, keeping company with the wildest lads about the parish. That Dick Royston especially, whose honesty was doubtful, but who, being a clever fellow, was a sort of leader, was doing great harm by setting his face against the new parson, and laughing at the boys who went to him. Mrs. King was very unhappy. It was almost worse to think of Harold than of his sick brother; and Alfred grieved very much too, and took to himself the blame of having made home miserable to Harold, and driven him into bad company; of having been so peevish and unpleasant, that it was no wonder he would not come near him more than could be helped; and above all, of having set a bad example of idleness and recklessness, when he was well. If the tears were brought into his eyes at first by some unkind neglect of Harold's, they were sure to end in this thought at last; and then the only comfort was, that Mr. Cope had told him that he might make his sick-bed very precious to his brother's welfare, by praying always for him.

Mr. Cope had talked it over with Mrs. King; and they had agreed that as Harold was under the regular age for Confirmation, and seemed so little disposed to prepare for it in earnest, they would not press it on him. He was far from fit for it, and he was in such a mood of impatient irreverence, that Mr. Cope was afraid of making his sin worse by forcing serious things on him, and his mother was in constant fear of losing her last hold on him.

Yet Harold was not a bad or unfeeling boy by nature; and if he would but have paused to think, he would have been shocked to see how cruelly he was paining his widowed mother and dying brother, just when he should have been their strength and stay.

One afternoon in October, when Alfred was in a good deal of pain, Mr. Blunt said he would send out some cooling ointment for the wound at the joint, when Harold took the evening letters into Elbury. Alfred reckoned much on the relief this was to give, and watched the ticks of the clock for the time for Harold to set off.

'Make haste,' were the last words his mother spoke—and Harold fully meant to make haste; nor was it weather to tempt him to stay long, for there was a chill raw fog hanging over the meadows, and fast turning into rain, which hung in drops upon his eyebrows, and the many-tiered cape of his father's box-coat, which he always wore in bad weather. It was fortunate he was likely to meet nothing, and that he and the pony both knew the road pretty well.

How fuzzy the grey fog made the lamps of the town look! Did they disturb the pony? What a stumble! Ha! there's a shoe off. Be it known that it was Harold's own fault; he had not looked at the shoes for many a morning, as he knew it was his duty to do.

He left Peggy with her ears back, much discomposed at being shod in a strange forge, and by any one but Bill Saunders.

Then Harold was going to leave his bag at the post-office, when, as he turned up the street, some one caught hold of him, and cried, 'Ho! Harold King on foot! What's the row? Old pony tumbled down dead?'

'Cast a shoe,' said Harold.

'Oh, jolly, you'll have to wait!' went on Dick Royston. 'Come in here! Here's such a lark!'

Harold looked into a court-yard belonging to a low public-house, and saw what was like a tent, with a bright red star on a blue ground at the end, lighted up. A dark figure came between, and there was a sudden crack that made Harold start.

'It's the unique (he called it eu-ni-quee) royal shooting-gallery, patronized by his Royal Highness the Prince of Wales,' (what a story!) said Dick. 'You've only to lay down your tin; one copper for three shots, and if you hit, you may take your choice—gingerbread-nuts, or bits of cocoa-nut, or, what's jolliest, lollies with gin inside 'em! Come, blaze away! or ha'n't you got the money? Does Mother keep you too short?'

If there was a thing Harold had a longing for, it was to fire off a gun! If there was a person he envied more than another, it was old Isaac Coffin, when he prowled up and down Farmer Ledbitter's fields with an old blunderbuss and some powder, to keep off the birds!

To be sure it was a public-house, but it was not inside one! And Mother would call it gambling. Oh, but it wasn't cards or skittles! And if he shot away his half-pence, how should he pay for the shoeing of the pony? The blacksmith might trust him, or the clerk at the post-office would lend him the money, or Betsey Hardman. And the time? One shot would not waste much! Pony must be shod. Besides, Dick and all the rest would say he was a baby.

He paid the penny, threw aside his cap, and took the gun, though after all it was only a sham one, and what a miss he made! What business had every one to set up that great hoarse laugh? which made him so angry that he had nearly turned on Dick and cuffed him for his pains.

However, he was the more bent on trying again, and the owner of the gallery shewed him how to manage better. He hit anything but the middle of the star, and just saw how he thought he might hit next time. Next time was barely a miss, so that the man actually gave him a gin-drop to encourage him. That made him mad to meet with real success; but it was the turn of another 'young gent,' as the man called him, and Harold had to stand by, with his penny in his hand, burning with impatience, and fancying he could mend each shot of that young gent, and another, and another, and another, who all thrust in to claim their rights before him. His turn came at last; and so short and straight was the gallery, that he really did hit once the side of the star, and once the middle, and thus gained one gingerbread-nut, and three of the gin-drops.

It would have been his nature to share them with Alfred, but he could not do so without saying where he had been, and that he could not do, so he gave one to Dick, and swallowed the rest to keep out the cold.

Just then the town clock struck six, and frightened him. He had been there three-quarters of an hour. What would they say at the post-office?

The clerk looked out of his hole as angry as clerk could look. 'This won't do, King,' he said. 'Late for sorting! Fine, remember—near an hour after time.'

'Pony cast a shoe, Sir,' said Harold. He had never been so near a downright falsehood.

'Whew! Then I suppose I must not report you this time! But look out! You're getting slack.'

No time this for borrowing of the clerk. Harold was really frightened, for he *had* dawdled much more than he ought of late, and though he sometimes fancied himself sick of the whole post business, a complaint to his mother would be a dreadful matter. It put everything else out of his head; and he ran off in great haste to get the money from Betsey Hardman, knocking loud at her green door.

What a cloud of steamy heat the room was, with the fire glowing like a red furnace, and five black irons standing up before it; and clothes-baskets full of heaps of whiteness, and horses with vapoury webs of lace and cambric hanging on them; and the three ironing-boards, where smoothness ran along with the irons; and the heaps of folded clothes; and Betsey in her white apron, broad and red in the midst of her maidens!

'Ha! Harold King! Well, to be sure, you are a stranger! Don't come nigh that there hoss; it's Mrs. Parnell's best pocket-handkerchiefs, real Walencines!' (she meant Valenciennes.) 'If you'll just run up and see Mother, I'll have it out of the way, and we'll have a cup of tea.'

'Thank you, but I—'

'My! What a smoke ye're in! Take care, or I shall have 'em all to do over again. Go up to Mother, do, like a good lad.'

'I can't, Betsey; I must go home.'

'Ay! that's the way. Lads never can sit down sensible and comfortable! it's all the same—'

'I wanted,' said Harold, interrupting her, 'to ask you to lend me sixpence. Pony's cast a shoe, and I had to leave her with the smith.'

'Ay? Who did you leave her with?'

'The first I came to, up in WoodStreet.'

'Myers. Ye shouldn't have done that. His wife's the most stuck-up proud body I ever saw—wears steel petticoats, I'll answer for it. You should have gone to Charles Shaw.'

'Can't help it,' said Harold. 'Please, Betsey, let me have the sixpence; I'll pay you faithfully to-morrow!'

'Ay! that's always the way. Never come in unless ye want somewhat. 'Twasn't the way your poor father went on! He'd a civil word for every one. Well, and can't you stop a minute to say how your poor brother is?'

'Much the same,' said Harold impatiently.

'Yes, he'll never be no better, poor thing! All decliny; as I says to Mother, what a misfortune it is upon poor Cousin King! they'll all go off, one after t'other, just like innocents to the slaughter.'

This was not a cheerful prediction; and Harold petulantly said he must get back, and begged for the sixpence. He got it at last, but not till all Betsey's pocket had been turned out; and finding nothing but shillings and threepenny-bits, she went all through her day's expenses aloud, calling all her girls to witness to help her to account for the sixpence that ought to have been there.

Mrs. Brown had paid her four and sixpence—one florin and a half-crown—and she had three threepenny-pieces in her pocket, and twopence. Then Sally had been out and got a shilling's-worth of soap, and six-penn'orth of blue, and brought home one shilling; and there was the sausages—no one could recollect what they had cost, though they talked so much about their taste; and five-pence-worth of red-herrings, and the butter; yes, and threepence to the beggar who said he had been in Sebastopol. Harold's head was ready to turn round before it was all done; but he got away at last, with a scolding for not going up to see Mother.

Home he trotted as hard as the pony would go, holding his head down to try to bury nose and mouth in his collar, and the thick rain plastering his hair, and streaming down the back of his neck. What an ill-used wretch was he, said he to himself, to have to rattle all over the country in such weather!

Here was home at last. How comfortable looked the bright light, as the cottage door was thrown open at the sound of the horse's feet!

'Well, Harold!' cried Ellen eagerly, 'is anything the matter?'

'No,' he said, beginning to get sulky because he felt he was wrong; 'only Peggy lost a shoe—'

'Lame?'

'No, I took her to the smith.'

'Give me Alfred's ointment, please, before you put her up. He is in such a way about it, and we can't put him to bed—'

'Haven't got it.'

'Not got it! O Harold!'

'I should like to know how to be minding such things when pony loses a shoe, and such weather! I declare I'm as wet—!' said Harold angrily, as he saw his sister clasp her hands in distress, and the tears come in her eyes.

'Is Harold come safe?' called Mrs. King from above.

'Is the ointment come?' cried Alfred, in a piteous pain-worn voice.

Harold stamped his foot, and bolted to the stable to put the pony away.

'It's not come,' said Ellen, coming up-stairs, very sadly.

'He has forgot it.'

'Forgot it!' cried Alfred, raising himself passionately. 'He always does forget everything! He don't care for me one farthing! I believe he wants me dead!'

'This is very bad of him! I didn't think he'd have done it,' said Mrs. King sorrowfully.

'He's been loitering after some mischief,' exclaimed Alfred. 'Taking his pleasure—and I must stay all this time in pain! Serve him right to send him back to Elbury.'

Mrs. King had a great mind to have done so; but when she looked at the torrents of rain that streamed against the window, and thought how wet Harold must be already, and of the fatal illnesses that had been begun by being exposed to such weather, she was afraid to venture a boy with such a family constitution, and turning back to Alfred, she said, 'I am very sorry, Alfred, but it can't be helped; I can't send Harold out in the rain again, or we shall have him ill too.'

Poor Alfred! it was no trifle to have suffered all day, and to be told the pain must go on all night. His patience and all his better thoughts were quite worn away, and he burst into tears of anger and cried out that it was very hard—his mother cared for Harold more than for him, and nobody minded it, if he lay in such pain all night.

'You know better than that, dear,' said his poor mother, sadly grieved, but bearing it meekly. 'Harold shall go as soon as can be to-morrow.'

'And what good will that be to-night?' grumbled Alfred. 'But you always did put Harold before me. However, I shall soon be dead and out of your way, that's all!'

Mrs. King would not make any answer to this speech, knowing it only made him worse. She went down to see about Harold, an additional offence to Alfred, who muttered something about 'Mother and her darling.'

'How can you, Alfred, speak so to Mother?' cried Ellen.

'I'm sure every one is cross enough to me,' returned Alfred.

'Not Mother,' said Ellen. 'She couldn't help it.'

'She won't send Harold out again, though; I'm sure I'd have gone for him.'

'You don't know what the rain was,' said Ellen.

'Well, he should have minded; but you're all against me.'

'You'll be sorry by-and-by, Alfred; this isn't like the way you talk sometimes.'

'Some one else had need to be sorry, not me.'

Perhaps, in the midst of his captious state, Alfred was somewhat pacified by hearing sounds below that made him certain that Harold was not escaping without some strong words from his mother.

They were not properly taken. Harold was in no mood of repentance, and the consciousness that he had been behaving most unkindly, only made him more rough and self-justifying.

'I can't help it! I can't be a slave to run about everywhere, and remember everything—pony losing her shoe, and nigh tumbling down with me, and Ross at the post so cross for nothing!'

'You'll grieve at the way you have used your poor brother one of these days, Harold,' quietly answered his mother, so low, that Alfred could not hear through the floor. 'Now, you'll please to go to bed.'

'Ain't I to have no supper?' said Harold in a sullen voice, with a great mind to sit down in the chimney-corner in defiance.

'I shall give you something hot when you are in bed. If I treated you as you deserve, I should send you to Mr. Blunt's this moment; but I can't afford to have you ill too, so go to bed this moment.'

His mother could still master him by her steadiness and he went up, muttering that he'd no notion of being treated like a baby, and that he would soon shew her the difference: he wasn't going to be made a slave to Alfred, and 'twas all a fuss about that stuff!

He did fancy he said his prayers; but they could not have been real ones, for he was no softer when his mother came to his bedside with a great basin of hot gruel. He said he hated such nasty sick stuff, and grunted savagely when, with a look that ought to have gone to his heart, she asked if he thought he deserved anything better.

Yet she did not know of the shooting gallery, nor of his false excuses. If he had not been deceiving her, perhaps he might have been touched.

'Well, Harold,' she said at last, after taking the empty basin from him, and picking up his wet clothes and boots to dry them by the fire, 'I hope as you lie there you'll come to a better mind. It makes me afraid for you, my boy. It is not only your brother you are sinning against, but if you are a bad boy, you know Who will be angry with you. Good-night.'

She lingered, but Harold was still hard, and would neither own himself sorry, nor say good-night.

When she passed his bed at the top of the stairs again, after hanging up the things by the fire, he had his head hidden, and either was, or feigned to be, asleep.

Alfred's ill-temper was nearly gone, but he still thought himself grievously injured, and was at no pains to keep himself from groaning and moaning all the time he was being put to bed. In fact, he rather liked to make the most of it, to shew his mother how provoking she was, and to reproach Harold for his neglect.

The latter purpose he did not effect; Harold heard every sound, and consoled himself by thinking what an intolerable work Alfred was making on purpose. If he had tried to bear it as well as possible, his brother would have been much more likely to be sorry.

Alfred was thinking too much about his misfortunes and discomforts to attend to the evening reading, but it soothed him a little, and the pain was somewhat less, so he did fall asleep, so uneasily though, that Mrs. King put off going to bed as late as she could.

It was nearly eleven, and Ellen had been in bed a long time, when Alfred started, and Mrs. King turned her head, at the click of the wicket gate, and a step plashing on the walk. She opened the little window, and the gust of wet wind puffed the curtains, whistled round the room, and almost blew out the candle.

'Who's there?

'It's me, Mrs. King! I've got the stuff,' called a hoarse tired voice.

'Well, if ever! It's Paul Blackthorn!' exclaimed Mrs. King. 'Thank ye kindly. I'll come and let you in.'

'Paul Blackthorn!' cried Alfred. 'Been all the way to Elbury for me! O Mother, bring him up, and let me thank him! But how ever did he know?' The tears came running down Alfred's cheeks at such kindness from a stranger. Mrs. King had hurried down-stairs, and at the threshold stood a watery figure, holding out the gallipot.

'Oh! thank you, thank you; but come in! Yes, come in! you must have something hot, and get dried.'

Paul shambled in very foot-sore. He looked as if he were made of moist mud, and might be squeezed into any shape, and streams of rain were dropping from each of his many rags.

'Well, I don't know how to thank you—such a night! But he'll sleep easy now. How did you come to think of it?'

'I was just coming home from the parson's, and I met Harold putting up Peggy, in a great way because he'd forgotten. That's all, Missus,' said Paul, looking shamefaced. 'Good-night to you.'

'No, no, that won't do. I must have you sit down and get dry,' said Mrs. King, nursing up the remains of the fire; and as Paul's day-garments served him for night-gear likewise, he could hardly help accepting the invitation, and spreading his chilled hands to the fire.

As to Mrs. King's feelings, it must be owned that, grateful as she was, it was rather like sitting opposite to the heap in the middle of Mr. Shepherd's farm-yard.

'Would you take that?' she said, holding out a three-penny piece. 'I'd make it twice as much if I could, but times are hard.'

'No, no, Missus, I didn't do it for that,' said Paul, putting it aside.

'Then you must have some supper, that I declare.'

And she brought out a slice of cold bacon, and some bread, and warmed some beer at the fire. She would go without bacon and beer herself to-morrow, but that was nothing to her. It was a real pleasure to see the colour come into Paul's bony yellow cheeks at the hearty meal, which he could not refuse; but he did not speak much, for he was tired out, and the fire and the beer were making him very sleepy.

Alfred rapped above with the stick that served as a bell. It was to beg that Paul would come and be thanked; and though Mrs. King was a little afraid of the experiment, she did ask him to walk up for a moment.

Grunt went he, and in rather an unmannerly way, he said, 'I'd rathernot.'

'Pray do,' said Mrs. King; 'I don't think Alfred will sleep easy without saying thank you.'

So Paul complied, and in a most ungainly fashion clumped up-stairs and stood at the door. He had not forgotten his last reception, and would not come a step farther, though Alfred stretched out his hand and begged him to come in.

Alfred could say only 'Thank you, I never thought any one would be so kind.'

And Paul made gruff reply, 'Ye're very welcome,' turned about as if he were running away, and tumbled down-stairs, and out of the house, without even answering Mrs. King's 'Good-night.'

Harold had wakened at the sounds. He heard all, but he chose to seem to be asleep, and, would you believe it? he was only the more provoked! Paul's exertion made his neglect seem all the worse, and he was positively angry with him for 'going and meddling, and poking his nose where he'd no concern. Now he shouldn't be able to get the stuff to-morrow, and so make it up; and of course mother would go and dock Paul's supper out of his dinner!'

If such reflections were going on upon one side of the partition, there were very different thoughts upon the other. The stranger's kindness had done more than relieve Alfred's pain: the warm sense of thankfulness had softened his spirit, and carried off his selfish fit. He knew not how kind people were to him, and how ungrateful he had been to punish his innocent mother and sister, and so much to magnify a bit of thoughtlessness on Harold's part; to be angry with his mother for not driving him out when she thought it might endanger his health and life, and to say such cruel things on purpose to wound her. Alfred felt himself far more cruel than he had even thought Harold.

And was this his resolution? Was this the shewing the sincerity of his repentance through his conduct in illness? Was this patience? Was it brotherly love? Was it the taking up the cross so as to bear it like his Saviour, Who spoke no word of complaining, no murmur against His tormentors?

How he had fallen! How he had lost himself! It was a bitter distress, and threw him almost into despair. He prayed over and over to be forgiven, and began to long for some assurance of pardon, and for something to prevent all his right feelings and wishes from thus seeming to slip away from his grasp at the first trial.

He told his mother how sorry he was; and she answered, 'Dear lad, don't fret about it. It was very hard for you to bear, and you are but learning, you see, to be patient.'

'But I'm not learning if I don't go on no better,' sighed Alfred.

'By bits you are, my boy,' she said; 'you are much less fractious now than you used to be, only you could not stand this out-of-the-way trial.'

Alfred groaned.

'Do you remember what our Saviour said to St. Peter?' said his mother; '"Whither I go thou canst not follow Me now, but thou shalt follow Me afterwards." You see, St. Peter couldn't bear his cross then, but he went on doing his best, and grieving when he failed, and by-and-by he did bear it almost like his Master. He got to be made strong out of weakness.'

There was some comfort to Alfred in this; but he feared, and yet longed, to see Mr. Cope, and when he came, had scarcely answered his questions as to how he felt, before he said, 'O Sir, I've been a bad boy again, and so cross to them all!'

'O Sir,' said Ellen, who could not bear for him to blame himself, 'I'm sure it was no wonder—he's so distracted with the pain, and Harold getting idling, and forgetting to bring him the ointment. Why, even that vagabond boy was so shocked, that he went all the way to Elbury that very night for it. I told Alfred you'd tell him that anybody would be put out, and nobody would think of minding what he said.'

'Nobody, especially so kind a sister,' said Mr. Cope, smiling; 'but that is not what Alfred is thinking of.'

'No, Sir,' said Alfred; 'their being so good to me makes it all the worse.'

'I quite believe so; and you are very much disappointed in yourself.'

'Oh yes, Sir, just when I wanted to be getting patient, and more like—' and his eyes turned to the little picture, and filled with tears.

Mr. Cope said somewhat of what his mother had said that he was but a scholar in patience, and that he must take courage, though he had slipped, and pray for new strengthening and refreshing to go on in the path of pain his Lord had hallowed for him.

Perhaps the words reminded Alfred of the part of the Catechism where they occur, for he said, 'Oh, I wish I was confirmed! If I could but take the Holy Sacrament, to make me stronger, and sure of being forgiven—'

'You shall—before—' said Mr. Cope, speaking eagerly, but becoming choked as he went on. 'You are one whom the Church would own as ready and desirous to come, though you cannot be confirmed. You should at once—but you see I am not yet a priest; I have not the power to administer the Holy Communion; but I trust I shall be one in the spring, and then, Alfred—Or if you should be worse, I promise you that I would bring some one here. You shall not go without the Bread of Life.'

Alfred felt what he said to the depths of his heart, but he could not say anything but 'Thank you, Sir.'

Mr. Cope, still much moved, laid his hand upon that of the boy. 'So, Alfred, we prepare together. As I hope and long to prepare myself to have that great charge committed to me, which our Saviour Christ gave to His Apostles; so you prepare for the receiving of that Bread and that Cup which will more fully unite you to Him, and join your suffering to what He bore for you.'

'How shall I, Sir?' murmured Alfred.

'I will do my best to shew you,' said Mr. Cope; 'but your Catechism tells you best. Think over that last answer.'

Alfred's face lighted sweetly as he went over it. 'Why, that's what I can't help doing, Sir; I can't forget my faults, I'm so afraid of them; and I'm sure I do want to lead a new life, if I didn't keep on being so bad; and thinking about His dying is the best comfort I have. Nor I'm sure I don't bear ill-will to nobody, only I suppose it is not charity to run out at poor Mother and Ellen when one's put out.'

'Perhaps that is what you want to learn,' said Mr. Cope, 'and to get all these feelings deepened, and more earnest and steadfast. If the long waiting does that for you, it will be good, and keep you from coming lightly to the Holy Feast.'

'Oh, I could not do that!' exclaimed Alfred. 'And may I think that all my faults will be taken away and forgiven?'

'All you repent of, and bring in faith—'

'That is what they say at church in the Absolution,' said Alfred thoughtfully.

'Rather it is what the priest says to them,' said Mr. Cope; 'it is the applying the promise of forgiveness that our Saviour bought. I may not yet say those words with authority, Alfred, but I should like to hope that some day I may speak them to you, and bring rest from the weight at your heart.'

'Oh! I hope I may live to that!' said Alfred.

'You shall hear them, whether from me or from another,' said Mr. Cope, 'that is, if God will grant us warning. But you need not fear, Alfred, if you thoroughly repent, and put your full faith in the great Sacrifice that has been offered for your sins and the sins of all the world. God will take care of His child, and you already have His promise that He will give you all that is needful for your salvation.'

CHAPTER VIII—CONFIRMATION

If Harold had known all the consequences of his neglect, perhaps he would have been more sorry for it than as yet he had chosen to be.

The long walk and the warm beer and fire sent Paul to his hay-nest so heavy with sleep, that he never stirred till next morning he was wakened by Tom Boldre, the shuffler, kicking him severely, and swearing at him for a lazy fellow, who stayed out at night and left him to do his work.

Paul stumbled to his feet, quite confused by the pain, and feeling for his shoes in the dark loft. The shuffler scarcely gave him an instant to put them on, but hunted him down-stairs, telling him the farmer was there, and he would catch it.

It would do nobody any good to hear the violent way in which Mr. Shepherd abused the boy. He was a passionate man, and no good labourers liked to work with him because of his tongue. With such grown men as he had, he was obliged to keep himself under some restraint, but this only incited him to make up for it towards the poor friendless boy.

It was really nearly eight o'clock, and Paul's work had been neglected, which was enough to cause displeasure; and besides, Boldre had heard Paul coming home past eleven, and the farmer insisted on knowing what he had been doing.

Under all his rags, Paul was a very proud boy, and thus asked, he would not tell, but stood with his legs twisted, looking very sulky.

'No use asking him,' cried Mrs. Shepherd's shrill voice at the back door; 'why, don't ye hear that Mrs. Barker's hen-roost has been robbed by Dick Royston and two or three more on 'em?'

'I never robbed!' cried Paul indignantly.

'None of your jaw,' said the farmer angrily. 'If you don't tell me this moment where you've been, off you go this instant. Drinking at the Tankard, I'll warrant.'

'No such thing, Sir,' said Paul. 'I went to Elbury after some medicine for a sick person.'

Somehow he had a feeling about the house opposite, which would not let him come out with the name in such a scene.

'That's all stuff,' broke in Mrs. Shepherd, 'I don't believe one word of it! Send him off; take my advice, Farmer, let him go where he comes from; Ellen King told me he was out of prison.'

Paul flushed crimson at this, and shook all over. He had all but turned to go, caring for nothing more at Friarswood; but just then, John Farden, one of the labourers, who was carrying out some manure, called out, 'No, no, Ma'am. Sure enough he did go to Elbury to Dr. Blunt's. I was on the road myself, and I hears him. "Good-night," says I. "Good-night," says he. "Where be'est going?" says I. "To doctor's," says he, "arter some stuff for Alfred King."

'Yes,' said Paul, speaking more to Farden than to his master, 'and then Mrs. King gave me some supper, and that was what made me so late.'

'She ought to be ashamed of herself, then,' said Mrs. Shepherd spitefully, 'having a vagabond scamp like that drinking beer at her house at that time of night. How one is deceived in folks!'

'Well, what are you doing here?' cried the farmer, turning on Paul angrily; 'd'ye mean to waste any more of the day?'

So Paul was not turned off, and had to go straight to his work. It was well he had had so good a supper, for he had not a moment to snatch a bit of breakfast. It so happened that his work was to go with John Farden, who was carrying out the manure in the cart. Paul had to hold the horse, while John forked it out into little heaps in the field. John was a great big powerful man, with a foolish face, not a good workman, nor a good character, or he would not have been at that farm. He had either never been taught anything, or had forgotten it all; he never went near church; he had married a disreputable wife, and had two or three unruly children, who were likely to be the plagues of their parents and the parish, but not a whit did John heed; he did not seem to have much more sense than to work just enough to get food, lodging, beer, and tobacco, to sleep all night, and doze all Sunday. There was not any malice nor dishonesty in him; but it was terrible that a man with an immortal soul should live so nearly the life of the brute beasts that have no understanding, and should never wake to the sense of God or of eternity.

He was not a man of many words, and nothing passed for a long time but shouts of hoy, and whoa, and the like, to the horse. Paul went heavily on, scarce knowing what he was about; there was a stunned jaded feel about him, as if he were hunted and driven about, a mere outcast, despised by every one, even by the Kings, whose kindness had been his only ray of brightness. Not that his senses or spirits were alive enough even to be conscious of pain or vexation; it was only a dull dreary heedlessness what became of him next; and, quick clever boy as he had been in the Union, he did not seem to have a bit more sense, thought, or feeling, than John Farden.

John Farden was the first to break the silence: 'I wouldn't bide,' said he.

Paul looked up, and muttered, 'I have nowhere to go.'

'Farmer uses thee shameful,' repeated John. 'Why don't thee cut?'

Paul saw the smoke of Mrs. King's chimney. That had always seemed like a friend to him, but it came across him that they too thought him a runaway from prison, and he felt as if his only bond of fellowship was gone. But there was something else, too; and he made answer, 'I'll bide for the Confirmation.'

'Eh?' said John, 'what good'll that do ye?'

'Help me to be a good lad,' said Paul, who knew John Farden would not enter into any other explanation.

'Why, what'll they do to ye?'

'The Bishop will put his hand on me and bless me,' said Paul; and as he said the words there was hope and refreshment coming back. He was a child of God, if no other owned him.

'Whoy,' said Farden, much as he might have spoken to his horse, 'rum sort of a head thou'st got! Thee'll never go up to Bishop such a guy!'

'Can't help it,' said Paul rather sullenly; 'it ain't the clothes that God looks at.'

John scanned him all over, with his face looking more foolish than ever in the puzzle he felt.

'Well,' he said, 'and what wilt get by it?'

'God's grace to do right, I hope,' said Paul; then he added, out of his sad heart, 'It's bad enough here, to be sure. It would be a bad look-out if one hoped for nothing afterwards.'

Somehow John's mind didn't take in the notion of afterwards, and he did not go on talking to Paul. Perhaps there was a dread in his poor dull mind of getting frightened out of the deadly stupefied sleep it was bound in.

But that bit of talk had done Paul great good, by rousing him to the thought of what he had to hope for. There was the Confirmation nigh at hand, and then on beyond there was rest; and the words came into his mind, 'There the wicked cease from troubling, and there the weary are at rest.'

Poor, poor boy! He was very young to have such yearnings towards the grave, and well-nigh to wish he lay as near to it as Alfred King, so he might have those loving tender hands near him, those kind voices round him. Paul had gone through a great deal in these few months; and, used to good shelter and regular meals, he was less inured to bodily hardship than many a cottage boy. His utter neglect of his person was telling on him; he was less healthy and strong than he had been, and though high spirits, merriment, and the pleasure of freedom and independence, had made all light to him in the summer, yet now the cold weather, with his insufficient food and scanty clothing, was dulling him and deadening him, and hard work and unkind usage seemed to be grinding his very senses down. To be sure, when twelve o'clock came, he went up into the loft, ate his bit of dry bread, and said his prayers, as he had not been able to do in the morning, and that made him feel less forlorn and downcast for a little while; but then as he sat, he grew cold, and numb, and sleepy, and seemed to have no life in him, but to be moving like a horse in a mill, when Boldre called him down, and told him not to be idling there.

The theft in Mrs. Barker's poultry-yard was never traced home to any one, but the world did not the less believe Dick Royston and Jesse Rolt to have been concerned in it. Indeed, they had been drinking up some of their gains when Harold met them at the shooting-gallery: and Mrs. Shepherd would not put it out of her head that Paul Blackthorn was in the secret, and that if he did really go for the medicine as he said, it was only as an excuse for carrying the chickens to some receiver of stolen goods. She had no notion of any person doing anything out of pure love and pity. Moreover, it is much easier to put a suspicion into people's heads than out again; and if Paul's whole history and each day's doings had been proved to her in a court of justice, she would still have chiefly remembered that she had always thought ill of him, and that Ellen King had said he was a runaway convict, and so she would have believed him to the end.

Ellen had long ago forgotten that she had said anything of the kind; and though she still held her nose rather high when Paul was near, she would have answered for his honesty as readily as for that of her own brothers. But hers had not been the charity that thinketh no evil, and her idle words had been like thistle-down, lightly sent forth, but when they had lighted, bearing thorns and prickles.

Those thorns were galling poor Paul. Nobody could guess what his glimpses of that happy, peaceful, loving family were to him. They seemed to him like a softer, better kind of world, and he looked at their fair faces and fresh, well-ordered garments with a sort of reverence; a kind look or greeting from Mrs. King, a mere civil answer from Ellen, those two sights of the white spirit-looking Alfred, were like the rays of light that shone into his dark hay-loft. Sometimes he heard them singing their hymns and psalms on a Sunday evening, and then the tears would come into his eyes as he leant over the gate to listen. And, as if it was because Ellen kept at the greatest distance from him, he set more store by her words and looks than those of any one else, was always glad when she served him in the shop, and used to watch her on Sunday, looking as fresh as a flower in her neat plain dress.

And now to hear that she not only thought meanly of him, which he knew well enough, but thought him a thief, a runaway, and an impostor coming about with false tales, was like a weight upon his sunken spirits, and seemed to take away all the little heart hard usage had left him, made him feel as if suspicious eyes were on him whenever he went for his bit of bread, and took away all his peace in looking at the cottage.

He did once take courage to say to Harold, 'Did your sister really say I had run away from gaol?'

'Oh, nobody minds what our Ellen says,' was the answer.

'But did she say so?'

'I don't know, I dare say she did. She's so fine, that she thinks no one that comes up-stairs in dirty shoes worth speaking to. I'm sure she's the plague of my life—always at me.'

That was not much comfort for Paul. He had other friends, to be sure. All the boys in the place liked him, and were very angry with the way the farmer treated him, and greatly to their credit, they admired his superior learning instead of being jealous of it. Mrs. Hayward, the sexton's wife, the same who had bound up his hand when he cut it at harvest, even asked him to come in and help her boys in the evenings with what they had to prepare for Mr. Cope. He was not sorry to do so sometimes. The cottage was a slatternly sort of place, where he did not feel ashamed of himself, and the Haywards were mild good sort of folks, from whom he was sure never to hear either a bad or an unkind word; though he did not care for them, nor feel refreshed and helped by being with them as he did with the Kings.

John Farden, too, was good-natured to him, and once or twice hindered Boldre from striking or abusing him; he offered him a pipe once, but Paul could not smoke, and another time brought him out a pint of beer into the field. Mrs. Shepherd spied him drinking it from her upper window, and believed all the more that he got money somehow, and spent it in drink.

So the time wore on till the Confirmation, all seeming like one dull heavy dream of bondage; and as the weather became colder, the poor boy seemed to have no power of thinking of anything, but of so getting through his work as to avoid violence, to keep himself from perishing with cold, and not to hurt his chilblains more than he could help.

All his quick intellect and good instruction seemed to have perished away, and the last time he went to Mr. Cope's, he sat as if he were stupid or asleep, and when a question came to him, sat with his mouth open like silly Bill Pridden.

Mr. Cope knew him too well not to feel, as he wrote the ticket, that there were very few of whom he could so entirely from his heart say 'Examined and APPROVED,' as the poor lonely outcast foundling, Paul Blackthorn, who could not even tell whether he were fifteen, sixteen, or seventeen, but could just make sure that he had once been caned by old Mr. Haynes, who went away from the Union twelve years ago.

'Do you think you can keep the ticket safe if I give it you now, Paul?' asked Mr. Cope, recollecting that the cows might sup upon it like his Prayer-book.

Paul put his hands down to the bottom of his pockets. They were all one hole, and that sad lost foolish look came over his wan face again, and startled Mr. Cope.

The boys grinned, but Charles Hayward stepped forward. 'Please, Sir, let me take care of it for him.'

Mr. Cope and Paul both agreed, and Mr. Cope kept Charles for a moment to say, as he gave him a shilling, 'Look here, Charles, do you think you can manage to get that poor fellow a tolerable breakfast on Saturday before he goes? And if you could make him look a little more decent?'

Charles pulled his forelock and looked knowing. In fact, there was a little plot among these good-natured boys, and Harold King was in it too, though he was not of the Confirmation party, and said and thought he was very glad of it. He did not want to bind himself to be so very good. Silly boy; as if Baptism had not bound him already!

Mrs. Hayward put her head out as Paul passed her cottage, and called out, 'I say, you Paul, you come in to-morrow evening with our Charlie and Jim, and I'll wash you when I washes them.'

Good Mrs. Hayward made a mistake that the more delicate-minded Mrs. King would never have made. Perhaps if a pail of warm water and some soap had been set before Paul, he might actually have washed himself; but he was much too big and too shamefaced a lad to fancy sharing a family scrubbing by a woman, whatever she might do to her own sons. But considering the size of the Hayward cottage, and the way in which the family lived, this sort of notion was not likely to come into the head of the good-natured mother.

So she and her boys were much vexed when Paul did not make his appearance, and she made a face of great disgust when Charles said, 'Never mind, Mother, my white frock will hide no end of dirt.'

'I shall have to wash it over again before you can wear it, I know,' said Mrs. Hayward. 'Not as I grudges the trouble; he's a poor lost orphant, that it's a shame to see so treated.'

Mrs. Hayward did not know that she was bestowing the cup of cold water, as well as being literally ready to wash the feet of the poor disciple.

A clean body is a type and token of a pure mind; and though the lads of Friarswood did not quite perceive this, there was a feeling about them of there being something unnatural and improper, and a disgrace to Friarswood, in any one going up to the Bishop in such a condition as Paul. Especially, as Charles Hayward said, when he was the pick of the whole lot. Perhaps Charles was right, for surely Paul was single-hearted in his hope of walking straight to his one home, Heaven, and he had been doing no other than bearing his cross, when he so patiently took the being 'buffeted' when he did well, and faithfully served his froward master.

But Paul was not to escape the outward cleansing, and from one of the very last people from whom it would have been expected. He had just pulled his bed of hay down over him, and was trying to curl himself up so as to stop his teeth from chattering, with Cæsar on his feet, when the dog growled, and a great voice lowered to a gruff whisper, said, 'Come along, young un!'

'I'm coming,' cried Paul.

Though it was not Boldre's voice, it had startled him terribly; he was so much used to ill-treatment, that he expected a savage blow every moment.

But the great hand that closed on him, though rough, was not unkind.

'Poor lad, how he quakes!' said John Farden's voice. 'Don't ye be afeard, it's only me.'

'Nobody got at the horses?' cried Paul.

'No, no; only I ain't going to have you going up to yon big parson all one muck-heap! Come on, and make no noise about it.'

Paul did not very well know what was going to befall him, but he did not feel unsafe with John Farden, and besides, his lank frame was in the grasp of that big hand like a mouse in the power of a mastiff. So he let himself be hauled down the ladder, into an empty stall, where, behold, there was a dark lantern (which had been at bad work in its time), a pail, a brush, a bit of soap, and a ragged towel.

John laid hold of him much as Alfred in his page days used to do of Lady Jane's little dog when it had to be washed, but Puck had the advantage in keeping on his shaggy coat all the time, and in being more gently handled, whereas Farden scrubbed with such hearty good-will, that Paul thought his very skin would come off. But he had undergone the like in the workhouse, and he knew how to accommodate himself to it; and when his rough bath was over, though he was very sore, and stiff, and chilly, he really felt relieved, and more respectable than he had done for many months, only rather sorry he must put on his filthy old rags again; and he gave honest John more thanks than might have been expected.

The Confirmation was to be at eleven o'clock, at Elbury, and John had undertaken his morning's work, so that Mr. Shepherd grudgingly consented to spare him, knowing that all the other farmers of course did the same, and that there would be a cry of shame if he did not.

Paul had just found his way down the ladder in the morning, with thoughts going through his mind that to him this would be the coming of the Comforter, and he was sure he wanted comfort; and that for some hours of this day at least, he should be at peace from rude words and blows, when he heard a great confusion of merry voices and suppressed laughing, and saw the heads of some of the lads bobbing about near Mrs. King's garden.

Was it time already to set off, he wondered, looking up to the sun; but then those boys seemed to be in an uproarious state such as did not suit his present mood, nor did he think Mr. Cope would consider it befitting. He would have let them go by, feeling himself such a scare-crow as they might think a blot upon them; but he remembered that Charles Hayward had his ticket, and as he looked at himself, he doubted whether he should be let into a strange church.

'Paul! Paul Blackthorn!' called Harold, with a voice all aglee.

'Well!' said Paul, 'what do you want of me?'

'Come on, and you'll see.'

'I don't want a row. Is Charlie Hayward there? Just ask him for my card, and don't make a work.'

'He'll give it you if you'll come for it,' said Harold; and seeing there was no other chance, Paul slowly came. Harold led him to the stable, where just within the door stood a knot of stout hearty boys, snorting with fun, hiding their heads on each other's shoulders, and bending their buskined knees with merriment.

'Now then!' cried Charles Hayward, and he had got hold of the only button that held Paul's coat together.

Paul was bursting out with something, but George Grant's arms were round his waist, and his hands were fumbling at his fastenings. They were each one much stronger than he was now, and they drowned his voice with shouts of laughter, while as fast as one garment was pulled off, another was put on.

'Mind, you needn't make such a work, it bain't presents,' said George Grant, 'only we won't have them asking up at Elbury if we've saved the guy to bring in.'

'It is a present, though, old Betty Bushel's shirt,' said Charles Hayward. 'She said she'd throw it at his head if he brought it back again; but the frock's mine.'

'And the corduroys is mine,' said George Grant. 'My! they be a sight too big in the band! Run in, Harold, and see if your mother can lend us a pin.'

'And the waistcoat is my summer one,' said Fred Bunting. 'He's too big too; why, Paul, you're no better than a natomy!'

'Never mind, my white frock will hide it all,' said Charles, 'and here's Ned's cap for you. Oh! and it's poor Alfred's boots.'

Paul could not make up his mind to walk all the way in the boots, but to satisfy the boys he engaged to put them on as soon as they were getting to Elbury.

'My! he looks quite respectable,' cried Charles, running back a little way to look at him.

'I wonder if Mr. Cope will know him?' exclaimed Harold, jumping leap-frog fashion on George Grant's back.

'The maids will take him for some strange gentleman,' exclaimed Jem Hayward; 'and why, bless me, he's washed, I do declare!' as a streak of light from the door fell on Paul's visage.

'No, you don't mean it,' broke out Charles. 'Let's look! yes, I protest, why, the old grime between his eyes is gone after all. How did you manage that, Paul?'

Paul rather uneasily mumbled something about John Farden, and the boys clapped their hands, and shouted, so that Alfred, who well knew what was going on, raised himself on his pillow and laughed. It was rather blunt treatment for feelings if they were tender, but these were rough warm-hearted village boys, and it was all their good-nature.

'And where's the grub?' asked Charles importantly, looking about.

'Oh, not far off,' said Harold; and in another moment, he and Charles had brought in a black coffee-pot, a large mug, some brown sugar, a hunch of bread, some butter, and a great big smoking sausage.

Paul looked at it, as if he were not quite sure what to do with it. One boy proceeded to turn in an inordinate quantity of sugar, another to pour in the brown coffee that sent out a refreshing steam enough to make any one hungry. George Grant spread the butter, cut the sausage in half, put it on the bread, and thrust it towards Paul.

'Eat it—s—s,' said Charles, patting Paul on the back. 'Mr. Cope said you was to, and you must obey your minister.'

'Not all for me?' said Paul, not able to help a pull at the coffee, the mug warming his fingers the while.

'Oh yes, we've all had our breakfastisses,' said George Grant; 'we are only come to make you eat yours like a good boy, as Mr. Cope said you should.'

They stood round, looking rather as they would have done had Paul been an elephant taking his meal in a show; but not one would hear of helping him off with a crumb out of Mr. Cope's shilling. George Grant was a big hungry lad, and his breakfast among nine at home had not been much to speak of; but savoury as was the sausage, and perfumy as was the coffee, he would have scorned to take a fragment from that stranger, beg him to do so as Paul might; and what could not be eaten at that time, with a good pint of the coffee, was put aside in a safe nook in the stable to be warmed up for supper.

That morning's work was not a bad preparation for Confirmation after all.

Harold had stayed so long, that he had to jump on the pony and ride his fastest to be in time at the post. He was very little ashamed of not being among those lads, and felt as if he had the more time to enjoy himself; but there were those who felt very sad for him—Alfred, who would have given so much to receive the blessing; and Ellen, whose confirmation was very lonely and melancholy without either of her brothers; besides his mother, to whom his sad carelessness was such constant grief and heart-ache.

Ellen was called for by the carriage from the Grange, and sat up behind with the kitchen-maid, who was likewise to be confirmed. Little Miss Jane sat inside in her white dress and veil, looking like a snowdrop, Alfred thought, as his mother lifted him up to the window to see her, as the carriage stood still while Ellen climbed to her seat.

In the course of the morning, Mrs. King made time to read over the Confirmation Service with Alfred, to think of the blessing she was receiving, and to pray that it might rest upon her through life. And they entreated, too, that Harold might learn to care for it, and be brought to a better mind.

'O Mother,' said Alfred, after lying thinking for sometime, 'if I thought Harold would take up for good and be a better boy to you than I have been, I should not mind anything so much.'

And there was Harold all the time wondering whether he should be able to get out in the evening to have a lark with Dick and Jesse.

Ellen was set down by-and-by. Her colour was very deep, but she looked gentle and happy, and the first thing she did was to bend over Alfred, kiss him, and say how she wished he had been there.

Then, when she had been into her own room, she came back and told them about the beautiful large Elbury Church, and the great numbers of young girls and boys on the two sides of the aisle, and of the Bishop seated in the chair by the altar, and the chanted service, with the organ sounding so beautiful.

And then how her heart had beat, and she hardly dared to speak her vow, and how she trembled when her turn came to go up to the rail, but she said it was so comfortable to see Mr. Cope in his surplice, looking so young among the other clergymen, and coming a little forward, as if to count out and encourage his own flock. She was less frightened when she had met his kind eye, and was able to kneel down with a more quiet mind to receive the gift which had come down on the Day of Pentecost.

Alfred wanted to know whether she had seen Paul, but Ellen had been kneeling down and not thinking of other people, when the Friarswood boys went up. Only she had passed him on the way home, and seen that though he was lagging the last of the boys, he did not look dull and worn, as he had been doing lately.

Ellen had been asked to go to the Grange after church to-morrow evening, and drink tea there, in celebration of the Confirmation which the two young foster-sisters had shared.

Harold went to fetch her home at night, and they both came into the house fresh and glowing with the brisk frosty air, and also with what they had to tell.

'O mother, what do you think? Paul Blackthorn is to go to the Grange to-morrow. My Lady wants to see him, and perhaps she will make Mr. Pound find some work for him about the farm.'

Harold jumped up and snapped his fingers towards the farm. 'There's for old Skinflint!' said he; 'not a chap in the place but will halloo for joy!'

'Well, I am glad!' said Mrs. King; 'I didn't think that poor lad would have held out much longer, winter weather and all. But how did my Lady come to hear of it?'

'Oh, it seems she noticed him going to church in all his rags, and Mr. Cope told her who he was; so Miss Jane came and asked me all about him, and I told her what a fine scholar he is, and how shamefully the farmer and Boldre treat him, and how good he was to Alfred about the ointment, and how steady he is. And I told her about the boys dressing him up yesterday, and how he wouldn't take a gift. She listened just as if it was a story, and she ran away to her grandmamma, and presently came back to say that the boy was to come up to-morrow after his work, for Lady Jane to speak to him.'

'Well, at least, he has been washed once,' said Mrs. King; 'but he's so queer; I hope he will have no fancies, and will behave himself.'

'I'll tackle him,' declared Harold decidedly. 'I've a great mind to go out this moment and tell him.'

Mrs. King prevented this; she persuaded Harold that Mrs. Shepherd would fly out at them if she heard any noise in the yard, and that it would be better for every one to let Paul alone till the morning.

Morning came, and as soon as Harold was dressed, he rushed to the farm-yard, but he could not find Paul anywhere, and concluded that he had been sent out with the cows, and would be back by breakfast-time.

As soon as he had brought home the post-bag, he dashed across the road again, but came back in a few moments, looking beside himself.

'He's gone!' he said, and threw himself back in a chair.

'Gone!' cried Mrs. King and Ellen with one voice, quite aghast.

'Gone!' repeated Harold. 'The farmer hunted him off this morning! Missus will have it that he's been stealing her eggs, and that there was a lantern in the stable on Friday night; so they told him to be off with him, and he's gone!'

'Poor, poor boy! just when my Lady would have been the making of him!' cried Ellen.

'But where—which way is he gone?' asked Mrs. King.

'I might ride after him, and overtake him,' cried Harold, starting up, 'but I never thought to ask! And Mrs. Shepherd was ready to pitch into me, so I got away as soon as I could. Do you run over and ask, Ellen; you always were a favourite.'

They were in such an eager state, that Ellen at once sprang up, and hastily throwing on her bonnet, ran across the road, and tapped at Mrs. Shepherd's open door, exclaiming breathlessly, 'O Ma'am, I beg your pardon, but will you tell me where Paul Blackthorn is gone?'

'Paul Blackthorn! how should I know?' said Mrs. Shepherd crossly. 'I'm not to be looking after thieves and vagabonds. He's a come-by-chance, and he's a go-by-chance, and a good riddance too!'

'Oh but, Ma'am, my Lady wanted to speak to him.'

This only made Mrs. Shepherd the more set against the poor boy.

'Ay, ay, I know—coming over the gentry; and a good thing he's gone!' said she. 'The place isn't to be harbouring thieves and vagrants, or who's to pay the rates? My eggs are gone, I tell you, and who should take 'em but that lad, I'd like to know?'

'Them was two rotten nest-eggs as I throwed away when I was cleaning the stable.'

'Who told you to put in your word, John Farden?' screamed Mrs. Shepherd, turning on him. 'Ye'd best mind what ye're about, or ye'll be after him soon.'

'No loss neither,' muttered John, stopping to pick up his shovel.

'And you didn't see which way he was gone?' asked Ellen, looking from the labourer to the farmer's wife.

'Farmer sent un off or ever I come,' replied John, 'or I'd ha' gied un a breakfast.'

'I'm sure I can't tell,' said Mrs. Shepherd, with a toss of her head. 'And as to you, Ellen King, I'm surprised at you, running after a scamp like that, that you told me yourself was out of a prison.'

'Oh but, Mrs. Shepherd—'

'You ought to be ashamed of yourself,' interrupted Mrs. Shepherd; 'and I wonder your mother allows it. But there's nothing like girls now-a-days.'

Ellen thought John Farden grinned; and feeling as if nothing so shocking could ever happen to her again, she flew back, she hardly knew how, to her home, clapped the door after, and dropping into a chair as Harold had done, burst into such a fit of crying, that she could not speak, and only shook her head in answer to Harold's questions as to how Paul was gone.

'Oh, no one knew!' she choked out among her sobs; 'and Mrs. Shepherd—such things!'

Harold stamped his foot, and Mrs. King tried to soothe her. In the midst, she recollected that she could not bear her brothers to guess at the worst part of the 'such things;' and recovering herself a moment, she said, 'No, no, they've driven him off! He's gone, and—and, oh! Mother, Mrs. Shepherd will have it he's a thief, and—and she says I said so.'

That was bad enough, and Ellen wept bitterly again; while her mother and Harold both cried out with surprise.

'Yes—but—I did say I dare said he was out of a reformatory—and that she should remember it! Now I've taken away his character, and he's a poor lost boy!'

Oh, idle words! idle words!

CHAPTER IX—ROBBING THE MAIL

There was no helping it! People must have their letters whether Paul Blackthorn were lost or not, and Harold was a servant of the public, and must do his duty, so after some exhortations from his mother, he ruefully rose up, hoping that he should not have to go to Ragglesford.

'Yes, you will,' said his mother, 'and maybe to wait. Here's a registered letter, and I think there are two more with money in them.'

'To think,' sighed Harold, as he mounted his pony, 'of them little chaps getting more money for nothing, than Paul did in a month by working the skin off his bones!'

'Don't be discontented, Harold, on that score. Them little chaps will work hard enough by-and-by: and the money they have now is to train them in making a fit use of it then.'

Harold looked anxiously up and down the road for Paul, and asked Mr. Cope's housekeeper whether he had been there to take leave. No; and indeed Harold would have been a little vexed if he had wished good-bye anywhere if not at home.

There was a fine white frost, and the rime hung thickly on every spray of the heavy branches of the dark firs and larches that overhung the long solitary lane between the Grange and Ragglesford, and fringed the park palings with crystals. Harold thought how cold poor Paul must be going on his way in his ragged clothes. The ice crackled under the pony's feet as she trotted down Ragglesford Lane, and the water of the ford looked so cold, that Peggy, a very wise animal, turned her head towards the foot-bridge, a narrow and not very sound affair, over which Harold had sometimes taken her when the stream was high, and threatened to be over his feet.

Harold made no objection; but no sooner were all the pony's four hoofs well upon the bridge, than at the other end appeared Dick Royston.

'Hollo, Har'ld!' was his greeting, 'I've got somewhat to say to ye.'

'D'ye know where Paul Blackthorn is?' asked Harold.

'Not I—I'm a traveller myself, you must know.'

'You, going to cut?' cried Harold.

'Ay,' said Dick, laying hold of the pony's rein. 'The police have been down at

Rolt's—stupid fellow left old gander's feet about—Mrs. Barker swore to 'em 'cause he'd had so many kicks and bites on common—Jesse's took up and peached—I've been hiding about all night—precious cold it was, and just waiting, you see, to wish you good-bye.'

Harold, very much shocked, could have dispensed with his farewells, nor did he like the look of his eyes.

'Thank you, Dick; I'm sorry—I didn't think—but I'm after time—I wish you'd let go of Peggy.'

'So that's all you have to say to an old comrade!' said Dick; 'but, I say, Har'ld, I'm not going so. I must have some tin to take me to Portsmouth. I want to know what you've got in that there bag!'

'You won't have that; it's the post. Let go, Dick;' and he pushed the pony forward, but Dick had got her fast by the head. Harold looked round for help, but Ragglesford Lane was one of the loneliest places in the country. There was not a house for half a mile, and Lady Jane's plantations shut in the road on either side.

'I mean to have it,' said Dick, looking coolly up into his face; 'I mean to see if there's any of the letters with a half-sovereign in 'em, that you tell us about.'

'Dick, Dick, it would be robbing! For shame, Dick! What would become of Mother and me?'

'That's your look-out,' said Dick; and he stretched out his hand for the bag. He was four years older than Harold, and much stouter.

Harold, with a ready move, chucked the bag round to his back, and shouted lustily in hopes that there might be a keeper in the woods, 'Help! Thieves! He's robbing the post!'

Dick's hoarse laugh was all the answer. 'That'll do, my dear,' he said; 'now you'd best be quiet; I'd be loath to hurt you.'

For all answer, Harold, shouting all the time, dealt him a stroke right over the eyes and nose with his riding-switch, and made a great effort to force the pony on in hopes the blow might have made him slacken his hold. But though one moment Dick's arm was thrown over his watering eyes, the other hand held the bridle as firmly as ever, and the next instant his fist dealt Harold such a blow, as nearly knocked out all his breath. Setting his teeth, and swearing an oath, Dick was pouncing on the boy's arm, when from the road before them came bursting a meagre thing darting like a wild cat, which fell upon him, hallooing as loud as Harold.

Dick turned in fury, and let go the bridle. The pony backed in alarm. The new-comer was grappling with the thief, and trying to drag him aside. 'On, on; go on, Har'ld!' he shouted, but his strength was far from equal to Dick's, who threw him aside on the hand-rail. Old rotten rail that it was, it crashed under the weight, and fell with both the boys into the water. Peggy dashed forward to the other side, where Harold pulled her up with much difficulty, and turned round to look at the robber and the champion. The fall was not far, nor the water deep, and they had both risen, and were ready to seize one another again in their rage. And now Harold saw that he who had come to his help was no other than Paul Blackthorn, who shouted loudly, 'On, go on! I'll keep him.'

'He'll kill you!' screamed Harold, in despair, ready to push in between them with his horse; but at that moment cart-wheels were heard in the road, and Dick, shaking his fist, and swearing at them both, shook off Paul as if he had been a feather, and splashing out of the ford on the other side, leapt over the hedge, and was off through the plantations.

Paul more slowly crept up towards Harold, dripping from head to foot.

'Paul! Paul! I'm glad I've found you!' cried Harold. 'You've saved the letters, man, and one was registered! Come along with me, up to the school.'

'Nay, I'll not do that,' said Paul.

'Then you'll stay till I come back,' said Harold earnestly; 'I've got so much to tell you! My Lady sent for you. Our Ellen told her all about you, and you're to go to her. Ellen was in such a way when she found you were off.'

'Then she didn't think I'd taken the eggs?' said Paul.

'She'd as soon think that I had,' said Harold. 'Why, don't we all know that you're one of the parson's own sort? But what made you go off without a word to nobody?'

'I don't know. Every one was against me,' said Paul; 'and I thought I'd just go out of the way, and you'd forget all about me. But I never touched those eggs, and you may tell Mr. Cope so, and thank him for all his kindness to me.'

'You'll tell him yourself. You're going home along with me,' cried Harold. 'There! I'll not stir a step till you've promised! Why, if you make off now, 'twill be the way to make them think you have something to run away for, like that rascal.'

'Very well,' said Paul, rather dreamily.

'Then you won't?' said Harold. 'Upon your word and honour?'

Paul said the words after him, not much as if he knew what he was about; and Harold, rather alarmed at the sound of the Grange clock striking, gave a cut to the pony, and bounded on, only looking back to see that Paul was seating himself by the side of the lane. Harold said to himself that his mother would not have liked to see him do so after such a ducking, but he knew that he was more tenderly treated than other lads, and with reason for precaution too; and he promised himself soon to be bringing Paul home to be dried and warmed.

But he was less speedy than he intended. When he arrived at the school, he had first to account to the servants for his being so late, and then he was obliged to wait while the owner of the registered letter was to sign the green paper, acknowledging its safe delivery.

Instead of having the receipt brought back to him, there came a message that he was to go up to tell the master and the young gentlemen all about the robbery.

So the servant led the way, and Harold followed a little shy, but more curious. The boys were in school, a great bare white-washed room, looking very cold, with a large arched window at one end, and forms ranged in squares round the hacked and hewed deal tables. Harold thought he should tell Alfred that the young gentlemen had not much the advantage of themselves in their schoolroom.

The boys were mostly smaller than he was, only those of the uppermost form being of the same size. There might be about forty of them, looking rather red and purple with the chilly morning, and all their eighty eyes, black or brown, blue or grey, fixed at once upon the young postman as he walked into the room, straight and upright, in his high stout gaiters over his cord trousers, his thick rough blue coat and red comforter, with his cap in his hand, his fair hair uncovered, and his blue eyes and rosy cheeks all the more bright for that strange morning's work. He was a well-mannered boy, and made his bow very properly to Mr. Carter, the master, who sat at his high desk.

'So, my little man,' said the master, 'I hear you've had a fight for our property this morning. You've saved this young gentleman's birthday present of a watch, and he wants to thank you.'

'Thank you, Sir,' said Harold; 'but he'd have been too much for me if Paul hadn't come to help. He's a deal bigger than me.'

The boys all made a thumping and scuffling with their feet, as if to applaud Harold; and their master said, 'Tell us how it was.'

Harold gave the account in a very good simple manner, only he did not say who the robber was—he did not like to do so—indeed, he would not quite believe it could be his old friend Dick. The boys clapped and thumped doubly when he came to the switching, and still more at the tumble into the water.

'Do you know who the fellow was?' asked Mr. Carter.

'Yes, I knowed him,' said Harold, and stopped there.

'But you had rather not tell. Is that it?'

'Please, Sir, he's gone, and I wouldn't get him into trouble.'

At this the school-boys perfectly stamped, and made signs of cheering.

'And who is the boy that came to help you?'

'Paul Blackthorn, Sir; he's a boy from the Union who worked at Farmer Shepherd's. He's a right good boy, Sir; but he's got no friends, nor no— nothing,' said Harold, pausing ere he finished.

'Why didn't you bring him up with you?' asked the master.

'Please, Sir, he wouldn't come.'

'Well,' said Mr. Carter, 'you've behaved like a brave fellow, and so has your friend; and here's something in token of gratitude for the rescue of our property.'

It was a crown piece.

'And here,' said the boy whose watch had been saved, 'here's half-a-crown. Shake hands, you're a jolly fellow; and I'll tell my uncle about you.'

Harold was a true Englishman, and of course his only answer could be, 'Thank you, Sir, I only did my duty;' and as the other boys, whose money had been rescued, brought forward more silver pledges of gratitude, he added, 'I'll take it to Paul—thank you, Sir—thank you, Sir.'

'That's right; you must share, my lad,' said the school-master. 'It is a reward for both of you.'

'Thank you, Sir, it was *my* duty,' repeated Harold, making his bow.

'Sir, Sir, pray let us give him three cheers,' burst out the head boy in an imploring voice.

Mr. Carter smiled and nodded; and there was such a hearty roaring and stamping, such 'hip, hip, hurrah!' bursting out again and again, that the windows clattered, and the room seemed fuller of noise than it could possibly hold. It is not quite certain that Mr. Carter did not halloo as loud as any of the boys.

Harold turned very red, and did not know which way to look while it was going on, nor what to do when it was over, except to say a very odd sort of

'Thank you, Sir;' but his heart leapt up with a kind of warm grateful feeling of liking towards those boys for going along with him so heartily; and the cheers gave a pleasure and glow that the coins never would have done, even had he thought them his own by right.

He was not particularly good in this; he had never felt the pinch of want, and was too young to care; and he did not happen to wish to buy anything in particular just then. A selfish or a covetous boy would not have felt as he did; but these were not his temptations. Knowing, as he did, that the assault had been the consequence of his foolish boasts about the money-letters, and that he, being in charge, ought to defend them to the last gasp, he was sure he deserved the very contrary from a reward, and never thought of the money belonging to any one but Paul, who had by his own free will come to the rescue, and saved the bag from robbery, himself from injury and disgrace.

How happy he was in thinking what a windfall it was for his friend, and how far it would go in fitting him up respectably!

Peggy was ready to trot nearly as fast as he wished her down the lane to the place where he had left Paul; and no sooner did Harold come in sight of the olive-coloured rags, than he bawled out a loud 'Hurrah! Come on, Paul; you don't know what I've got for you! 'Twas a young gentleman's watch as you saved; and they've come down right handsome! and here's twelve-and-sixpence for you—enough to rig you out like a regular swell! Why, what's the matter?' he added in quite another voice, as he had now come up to Paul, and found him sitting nearly doubled up, with his head bent over his knees.

He raised his face up as Harold came, and it was so ghastly pale, that the boy, quite startled, jumped off his pony.

'Why, old chap, what is it? Have you got knit up with cold, sitting here?'

'Yes, I suppose so,' said Paul; but his very voice shivered, his teeth chattered, and his knees knocked together with the chill. 'The pains run about me,' he added; but he spoke as if he hardly knew what he was doing or saying.

'You must come home with me, and Mother will give you something hot,' said Harold. 'Come, you'll catch your death if you don't. You shall ride home.'

He pulled Paul from his seat with some difficulty, and was further alarmed when he found that the poor fellow reeled and could hardly stand; but he was somewhat roused, and knew better what he was about. Harold tried to put him on the pony, but this could not be managed: he could not help himself enough, Peggy always swerved aside, nor was Harold strong enough to lift him up.

The only thing to be done was for Harold to mount, and Paul to lean against the saddle, while the pony walked. When they had to separate at the ford, poor Paul's walk across the bridge was so feeble and staggering, that Harold feared every moment that he would fall where the rail was broken away, but was right glad to put his arm on his shoulder again to help to hold him up. The moving brought a little more life back to the poor boy's limbs, and he walked a little better, and managed to tell Harold how he had felt too miserable to speak to any one after the rating the farmer had given him, and how he had set out on the tramp for more work, though with hope so nearly dead in his heart, that he only wished he could sit down and die. He had walked out of the village before people were about, so as not to be noticed, and then had found himself so weak and weary that he could not get on without food, and had sat down by the hedge to eat the bit of bread he had with him. Then he had taken the first lonely-looking way he saw, without knowing that it was one of Harold's daily rides, and was slowly dragging himself up the hill from the ford when the well-known voice, shouting for help, had suddenly called him back, and filled him with spirit and speed that were far enough off now, poor fellow!

That was a terrible mile and a half—Harold sometimes thought it would never be over, or that Paul would drop down, and he would have to gallop off for help; but Paul was not one to give in, and somehow they got back at last, and Harold, with his arm round his friend, dragged him through the garden, and across the shop, and pushed him into the arm-chair by the fire, Mrs. King following, and Ellen rushing down from up-stairs.

'There!' cried Harold, all in a breath, 'there he is! That rascal tried to rob me on Ragglesford Bridge, and was nigh too much for me; but *he* there came and pulled him off me, and got spilt into the river, and he's got a chill, and if you don't give him something jolly hot, Mother, he'll catch his death!'

Mrs. King thought so too: Paul's state looked to her more alarming than it did even to Harold. He did not seem able to think or speak, but kept rocking himself towards the fire, and that terrible shivering shaking him all over.

'Poor lad!' she said kindly. 'I'll tell you what, Harold, all you can do is put him into your bed at once.—Here, Ellen, you run up first, and bring me a shirt to warm for him. Then we'll get his own clothes dried.'

'No, no,' cried Harold, with a caper, 'we'll make a scare-crow of 'em. You don't know what I know, Mother. I've got twelve shillings and sixpence here all his own; and you'll see what I won't do with it at old Levi's, the second-hand clothes man, to-night.'

Harold grew less noisy as he saw how little good the fire was doing to his patient, and how ill his mother seemed to think him. He quietly obeyed her, by getting him up-stairs, and putting him into his own bed, the first in which Paul had lain down for more than four months. Then Mrs. King sent Harold out for some gin; she thought hot spirits and water the only chance of bringing back any life after such a dreadful chill; and she and Ellen kept on warming flannels and shawls to restore some heat, and to stop the trembling that shook the bed, so that Alfred felt it, even in the next room, where he lay with the door open, longing to be able to help, and wishing to understand what could have happened.

At last, the cordial and the warm applications effected some good. Paul was able to say, 'I don't know why you are so good to me,' and seemed ready to burst into a great fit of crying; but Mrs. King managed to stop him by saying something about one good turn deserving another, and that she hoped he was coming round now.

Harold was now at leisure to tell the story in his brother's room. Alfred did not grieve now at his brother's being able to do spirited things; he laughed out loud, and said, 'Well done, Harold!' at the switching, and rubbed his hands, and lighted up with glee, as he heard of the Ragglesford boys and their cheers; and then, Harold went eagerly on with his scheme for fitting up Paul at the second-hand shop, both Mrs. King and Alfred taking great interest in his plans, till Mrs. King hearing something like a moan, went back to Paul.

She found his cheeks and hands as burning hot as they had been cold; they were like live coals; and what was worse, such severe pains were running all over his limbs, that he was squeezing the clothes into his mouth that he might not scream aloud.

Happily it was Mr. Blunt's day for calling; and before the morning was over he came, and after a few words of explanation, he stood at Paul's bedside.

Not much given to tenderness towards the feelings of patients of his degree, Mr. Blunt's advice was soon given. 'Yes, he is in for rheumatic fever—won't be about again for a long time to come. I say, Mistress, all you've got to do is to send in your boy to the Union at Elbury, tell 'em to send out a cart for him, and take him in as a casual pauper. Then they may pass him on to his parish.'

Therewith Mr. Blunt went on to attend to Alfred.

'Then you think this poor lad will be ill a long time, Sir?' said Mrs. King, when Mr. Blunt was preparing to depart.

'Of course he will; I never saw a clearer case! You'd better send him off as fast as you can, while he can be moved. He'll have a pretty bout of it, I dare say.

'It is nothing infectious, of course, Sir?' said the mother, a little startled by this hastiness.

'Infectious—nonsense! why, you know better than that, Mrs. King; I only meant that you'd better get rid of him as quick as you can, unless you wish to set up a hospital at once—and a capital nurse you'd be! I would leave word with the relieving officer for you, but that I've got to go on to Stoke, and shan't be at home till too late.'

Mrs. King's heart ached for the poor forlorn orphan, when she remembered what she had heard of the nursing in Elbury Union. She did not know how to turn him from her door the day he had saved her son from danger such as she could not think of without shuddering; and yet, what could she do? Her rent and the winter before her, a heavy doctor's bill, and the loss of Alfred's work!

Slowly she went up the stairs again to the narrow landing that held the bed where Paul Blackthorn lay. He was quite still, but there were large tears coursing one after the other from his eyes, his hollow cheeks quite glazed with them.

'Is the pain so very bad?' she said in her soft voice, putting her hand over his hot forehead, in the way that Alfred liked.

'I don't—know,' he answered; and his black eyes, after looking up once in her face with the piteous earnest glance that some loving dogs have, shut themselves as if on purpose to keep in the tears, but she saw the dew squeezing out through the eye-lashes.

'My poor boy, I'm sure it's very bad for you,' she said again.

'Please, don't speak so kind,' said Paul; and this time he could not prevent a-sob. 'Nobody ever did so before, and—' he paused, and went on, 'I suppose they do it up in Heaven, so I hope I shall die.'

'You are vexing about the Union,' said Mrs. King, without answering this last speech, or she knew that she should begin to cry herself.

'I *did* think I'd done with them,' said Paul, with another sob. 'I said I'd never set foot in those four walls again! I was proud, maybe; but please don't stop with me! If you wouldn't look and speak like that, the place wouldn't seem so hard, seeing I'm bred to it, as they say;' and he made an odd sort of attempt to laugh, which ended in his choking himself with worse tears.

'Harold is not gone yet,' said Mrs. King soothingly; 'we'll wait till he comes in from his work, and see how you are, when you've had a little sleep. Don't cry; you aren't going just yet.'

That same earnest questioning glance, but with more hope in it, was turned on her again; but she did not dare to bind herself, much as she longed to take the wanderer to her home. She went on to her son's room.

'Mother, Mother,' Alfred cried in a whisper, so eager that it made him cough, 'you can't never send him to the workhouse?'

'I can't bear the thought, Alfy,' she said, the tears in her eyes; 'but I don't know what to do. It's not the trouble. That I'd take with all my heart, but it is hard enough to live, and—'

'I'm sure,' said Ellen, coming close, that her undertone might be heard, 'Harold and I would never mind how much we were pinched.'

'And I could go without—some things,' began Alfred.

'And then,' went on the mother, 'you see, if we got straitened, and Matilda found it out, she'd want to help, and I can't have her savings touched; and yet I can't bear to let that poor lad be sent off, so ill as he is, and after all he's done for Harold—such a good boy, too, and one that's so thankful for a common kind word.'

'O Mother, keep him!' said Alfred; 'don't you know how the Psalm says, "God careth for the stranger, and provideth for the fatherless and the widow"?'

Mrs. King almost smiled. 'Yes, Alf, I think it would be trusting God's word; but then there's my duty to you.'

'You've not sent Harold off for the cart?' said Alfred.

'No; I thought somehow, we have enough for to-day; and it goes against me to send him away at once. I thought we'd wait to see how it is to-morrow; and Harold won't mind having a bed made up in the kitchen.'

Tap, tap, on the counter. Some one had come in while they were talking. It was Mr. Cope, very anxious to hear the truth of the strange stories that were going about the place. Ellen and Alfred thought it very tiresome that he was so long in coming up-stairs; but the fact was, that their mother was very glad to talk the matter over without them. She knew indeed that Mr. Cope was a very young man, and not likely to be so well able as herself, with all her experience, to decide what she could afford, or whether she ought to follow her feelings at the risk of debt or of privations for her delicate children; but she also knew that though he had not experience, education had given him a wider and clearer range of thought; and that, as her pastor, he ought to be consulted; so though she did not exactly mean to make it a matter for his decision (unless, indeed, he should have some view which had not occurred to her), she knew that he was by far the best person to help her to see her way, and form her own judgment.

Mr. Cope heard all the story with as much eagerness as the Ragglesford boys themselves, and laughed quite out loud at Harold's spirited defence.

'That's a good lad!' said he. 'Well, Mrs. King, I don't think you need be very uneasy about your boy. When a fellow can stand up like that in defence of his duty, there must be the right stuff in him to be got at in time! And now, as to his ally—this other poor fellow—very kind of you to have taken him in.'

'I couldn't do no other, Sir,' said Mrs. King; 'he came in so drenched, and so terribly bad, I could do nothing but let him lie down on Harold's bed; and now Dr. Blunt thinks he's going to have a rheumatic fever, and wanted me to send in to the relieving officer, to have him removed, but I don't know how to do that; the poor lad doesn't say one word against it, but I can see it cuts him to the heart; and they do tell such stories of the nurses at the Union, that it does seem hard to send him there, such an innocent boy, too, and one that doesn't seem to know how to believe it if one says a kind word to him.' The tears were in Mrs. King's eyes as she went on: 'I do wish to let him stay here and do what I can for him, with all my heart, and so does all the children, but I don't hardly know what's right by them, poor things. If the parish would but allow him just one shilling and sixpence a week out of the house, I think I could do it.'

'What, with your own boy in such a state, you could undertake to nurse a stranger through a rheumatic fever!'

'It wouldn't make much difference, Sir,' said Mrs. King. 'You see I am up a good deal most nights with Alfred, and we have fire and candle almost always alight. I should only be glad to do it for a poor motherless lad like that, except for the cost; and I thought perhaps if you could speak to the Guardians, they might allow him ever so little, because there will be expenses.'

Mr. Cope had not much hope from the parish, so he said, 'Mr. Shepherd ought to do something for him after he has worked for him so long. He has been looking wretchedly ill for some time past; and I dare say half this illness is brought on by such lodging and living as he got there. But what did you say about some eggs?'

Mrs. King told him; and he stood a moment thoughtful, then said, 'Well, I'll go and see about it,' and strode across to the farm.

When Mr. Cope came back, Ellen was serving a customer. He stood looking redder than they had ever seen him, and tapping the toe of his boot impatiently with his stick; and the moment the buyer had turned away, he said, 'Ellen, ask your mother to be kind enough to come down.'

Mrs. King came, and found the young Curate in such a state of indignation, as he could not keep to himself. He had learnt more than he had ever known, or she had ever known, of the oppression that the farmer and his wife and Tom Boldre had practised on the friendless stranger, and he was burning with all the keen generous displeasure of one new to such base ways. At the gate he had met, going home to dinner, John Farden with Mrs. Hayward, who had been charing at the farm. Both had spoken out, and he had learned how far below the value of his labour the boy had been paid, how he had been struck, abused, and hunted about, as would never have been done to one who had a father to take his part. And he had further heard Farden's statement of having himself thrown away the eggs, and Mrs. Hayward's declaration that she verily believed that the farmer only made the accusation an excuse for hurrying the lad off because he thought him faltering for a fever, and wouldn't have him sick there.

This was shocking enough; Mr. Cope had thought it merely the kind-hearted woman's angry construction, but it was still worse when he came to the farmer and his wife.

So used were they to think it their business to wring the utmost they could out of whatever came in their way, that they had not the slightest shame about it. They thought they had done a thing to be proud of in making such a good bargain of the lad, and getting so much work out of him for so little pay; in fact, that they had been rather weakly kind in granting him the freedom of the hay-loft; the notion of his dishonesty was firmly fixed in their heads, though there was not a charge to bring against him. This was chiefly because they had begun by setting him down as a convict, and because they could not imagine any one living honestly on what they gave him. And lastly, the farmer thought the cleverest stroke of all, was the having got rid of him just as winter was coming on and work was scarce, and when there seemed to be a chance of his being laid up to encumber the rates. Mr. Cope was quite breathless after the answer he had made to them. He had never spoken so strongly in his life before, and he could hardly believe his own ears, that people could be found, not only to do such things, but to be proud of having done them.

It is to be hoped there are not many such thoroughgoing tyrants; but selfishness is always ready to make any one into a tyrant, and Mammon is a false god, who manages to make his servants satisfied that they are doing their duty.

It was plain enough that no help was to be expected from the farm, and neither Mrs. King nor the clergyman thought there was much hope in the Guardians; however, they were to be applied to, and this would be at least a reprieve for Paul. Mr. Cope went up to see him, and found Harold sitting on the top step of the stairs.

'Well, boys,' he said, in his hearty voice, 'so you've had a battle, I hear. I'm glad it turned out better than your namesake's at Hastings.'

Paul was not too ill to smile at this; and Harold modestly said, 'It was all along of he, Sir.'

'And he seems to be the chief sufferer.—Are you in much pain, Paul?'

'Sometimes, Sir, when I try to move,' said Paul; 'but it is better when I'm still.'

'You've had a harder time of it than I supposed, my boy,' said Mr. Cope. 'Why did you never let me know how you were treated?'

Paul's face shewed more wonder than anything else. 'Thank you, Sir,' he said, 'I didn't think it was any one's business.'

'No one's business!' exclaimed the young clergyman. 'It is every one's business to see justice done, and it should never have gone on so if you had spoken. Why didn't you?'

'I didn't think it would be any use,' again said Paul. 'There was old Joe Joiner, he always said 'twas a hard world to live in, and that there was nothing for it but to grin and bear it.'

'There's something better to be done than to grin,' said Mr. Cope.

'Yes, I know, Sir,' said Paul, with a brighter gleam on his face; 'and I seem to understand that better since I came here. I was thinking,' he added, 'if they pass me back to Upperscote, I'll tell old Joe that folks are much kinder than he told me, by far.'

'Kinder—I should not have thought that your experience!' exclaimed Mr. Cope, his head still running on the Shepherds.

But Paul did not seem to think of them at all, or else to take their treatment as a matter-of-course, as he did his Union hardships. There was a glistening in his eyes; and he moved his head so as to sign down-stairs, as he said, 'I didn't think there was ne'er a one in the world like *her*.'

'What, Mrs. King? I don't think there are many,' said Mr. Cope warmly. 'And yet I hope there are.'

'Ay, Sir,' said Paul fervently. 'And there's Harold, and John Farden, and all the chaps. Please, Sir, when I'm gone away, will you tell them all that I'll never forget 'em? and I'll be happier as long as I live for knowing that there are such good-hearted folks.'

Mr. Cope felt trebly moved towards one who thought harshness so much more natural than kindness, and who received the one so submissively, the other so gratefully; but the conversation was interrupted by Harold's exclaiming that my Lady in her carriage was stopping at the gate, and Mother was running out to her.

Rumours of the post-office robbery, as little Miss Selby called it, had travelled up to the Grange, and she was wild to know what had happened to Harold; but her grandmamma, not knowing what highway robbers might be roaming about Friarswood, would not hear of her walking to the post-office, and drove thither with her herself, in full state, close carriage, coachman and footman; and there was Mrs. King, with her head in at the carriage window, telling all the story.

'So you have this youth here?' said Lady Jane.

'Yes, my Lady; he was so poorly that I couldn't but let him lie down.'

'And you have not sent him to the workhouse yet?'

'Why, no, not yet, my Lady; I thought I would wait to see how he is to-morrow.'

'You had better take care, Mary,' said Lady Jane. 'You'll have him too ill to be moved; and then what will you do? a great lad of that age, and with illness enough in the house already!' She sighed, and it was not said unkindly; but Mrs. King answered with something about his being so good a lad, and so friendless. And Miss Jane exclaimed, 'O Grandmamma, it does seem so hard to send him to the workhouse!'

'Do not talk like a silly child, my dear,' said Lady Jane. 'Mary is much too sensible to think of saddling herself with such a charge—not fit for her, nor the children either—even if the parish made it worth her while, which it never will. The Union is intended to provide for such cases of destitution; and depend on it, the youth looks to nothing else.'

'No, my Lady,' said Mrs. King; 'he is so patient and meek about it, that it goes to one's very heart.'

'Ay, ay,' said the old lady; 'but don't be soft-hearted and weak, Mary. It is not what I expect of you, as a sensible woman, to be harbouring a mere vagrant whom you know nothing about, and injuring your own children.'

'Indeed, my Lady,' began Mrs. King, 'I've known the poor boy these four months, and so has Mr. Cope; and he is as steady and serious a boy as ever lived.'

'Very likely,' said Lady Jane; 'and I am sure I would do anything for him—

give him work when he is out again, or send him with a paper to the county hospital. Eh?'

But the county hospital was thirty miles off; and the receiving day was not till Saturday. That would not do.

'Well,' added Lady Jane, 'I'll drive home directly, and send Price with the spring covered cart to take him in to Elbury. That will be better for him than jolting in the open cart they would send for him.'

'Why, thank you, my Lady, but I—I had passed my word that he should not go to-day.'

Lady Jane made a gesture as if Mary King were a hopelessly weak good-natured woman; and shaking her head at her with a sort of lady-like vexation, ordered the coachman to drive on.

My Lady was put out. No wonder. She was a very sensible, managing woman herself, and justly and up-rightly kind to all her dependants; and she expected every one else to be sternly and wisely kind in the same pattern. Mrs. King was one whom she highly esteemed for her sense and good judgment, and she was the more provoked with her for any failure in these respects. If she had known Paul as the Kings did, it is probable she might have felt like them. Not knowing him, nor knowing the secrets of Elbury Union, she thought it Mrs. King's clear duty to sacrifice him for her children's sake. Moreover, Lady Jane had strict laws against lodgers—the greatest kindness she could do her tenants, though often against their will. So to have her model woman receiving a strange boy into her house, even under the circumstances, was beyond bearing.

So Mrs. King stood on her threshold, knowing that to keep Paul Blackthorn would be an offence to her best friend and patroness. Moreover, Mr. Cope was gone, without having left her a word of advice to decide her one way or the other.

CHAPTER X—CHRISTMAS DAY

Things are rather apt to settle themselves; and so did Paul Blackthorn's stay at the post-office, for the poor boy was in such an agony of pain all night, and the fever ran so high, that it was impossible to think of moving him, even if the waiting upon him in such suffering had not made Mrs. King feel that she could not dismiss him to careless hands. His patience, gratitude, and surprise at every trouble she took for him were very endearing, as were the efforts he made to stifle and suppress moans and cries that the terrible aches would wring from him, so as not to disturb Alfred. When towards morning the fever ran to his head, and he did not know what he said, it was more moving still to see that the instinct of keeping quiet for some one's sake still suppressed his voice. Then, too, his wanderings shewed under what dread and harshness his life had been spent, and what his horror was of a return to the workhouse. In his senses, he would never have thought of asking to remain at Friarswood; but in his half-conscious state, he implored again and again not to be sent away, and talked about not going back, but only being left in a corner to die; and Mrs. King, without knowing what she was about, soothed him by telling him to lie still, for he was not going to that place again. At day-break she sent Harold, on his way to the post, for an order from the relieving officer for medical attendance; and, after some long and weary hours, the Union doctor came. He said, like Mr. Blunt, that it was a rheumatic fever, the effect of hardship and exposure; for which perhaps poor Paul—after his regular meals, warm clothing, and full shelter, in the workhouse—was less prepared than many a country lad, whose days had been much happier, but who had been rendered more hardy by often going without some of those necessaries which were provided for the paupers.

The head continued so much affected, that the doctor said the hair must be taken off; which was done by old Master Warren, who singed the horses in the autumn, killed the pigs in the winter, and shaved the men on Saturday night. It was a very good thing for all parties; and he would take no pay for his trouble, but sent down a pitcher with what he called 'all manner of yarbs' steeping in it, with which, as he said, to 'ferment the boy's limbs.' Foment was what he meant; and Mrs. King thought, as it was kindly intended, and could do no harm, she would try if it would do any good; but she could not find that it made much difference whether she used that or common warm water. However, the good will made Paul smile, and helped to change his notion about its being very few that had any compassion for a stranger. So, too, did good Mrs. Hayward, who, when he was at the worst, twice came to sit up all night with him after her day's work; and though she was not as tender a nurse as Mrs. King, treated him like her own son, and moreover carried off to her own tub all the clothes she could find ready to be washed, and would not take so much as a mouthful of meat or drink in return, struggling, toil-worn body as she was.

The parish, as might have been foreseen, would afford nothing but the doctor to a chance-comer such as Paul. If he needed more, he might come into the House, and be passed home to Upperscote.

But by the time this reply came, Mrs. King not only felt that it would be almost murder to send a person in such a state four miles on a November day, but she was caring so much for her patient, that it sounded almost as impossible as to send Alfred away.

Besides, she had remembered the cup of cold water, she had thought of the widow's cruse of oil and barrel of meal, and she had called to mind, 'Inasmuch as ye have done it unto one of the least of these My brethren, ye have done it unto Me;' and thereupon she took heart, and made up her mind that it was right to tend the sick lad; and that even if she should bring trouble and want on herself and her children, it would be a Heaven-sent trial that would be good for them.

So she made up her resolution to a winter of toil, anxiety, and trouble, and to Lady Jane's withdrawal of favour; and thinking her ungrateful, which, to say the truth, grieved her more than anything else, excepting of course her forebodings for Alfred.

Ellen was in great distress about my Lady's displeasure. Not that she dreamt of her mother's giving up Paul on that account; but she was very fond of her little foster-sister, and of many of the maid-servants, and her visits to the Grange were the chief change and amusement she ever had. So while Mrs. King was busy between the shop, her work, and Paul, Ellen sat by her brother, making the housekeeper's winter dress, and imagining all sorts of dreadful things that might come of my Lady being angry with them, till Alfred grew quite out of patience. 'Well, suppose and suppose,' he said, 'suppose it was not to happen at all! Why, Mother's doing right would be any good for nothing if she only did it to please my Lady.'

Certainly this was the very touchstone to shew whether the fear of man were the guide. And Ellen was still more terrified that day, for when she went across to the farm for the evening's supply of milk and butter, Mrs. Shepherd launched out into such a torrent of abuse against her and her mother, that she came home trembling from head to foot; and Mrs. King declared she should never go thither again. They would send to Mrs. Price's for the little bit of fresh butter that was real nourishment to Alfred: the healthy ones would save by going without any.

One word more as to the Shepherds, and then we have done with him. On the Sunday, Mr. Cope had an elder brother staying with them, who preached on the lesson for the day, the second chapter of the Prophet Habakkuk; and when he came to the text, 'Woe to him that coveteth an evil covetousness to his house,' he brought in some of the like passages, the threats to those that 'grind the faces of the poor,' that 'oppress the hireling in his wages,' and that terrible saying of St. James, 'Behold, the hire of the labourers who have reaped down your fields, which is of you kept by fraud, crieth; and the cries of them which have reaped are entered into the ears of the Lord of Sabbath.'

Three days after, the Curate was very much amazed to hear that Mr. and Mrs. Shepherd did not choose to be preached at in their own church, and never meant to come thither again. Now it so happened that he could testify that the sermon had been written five years ago, and that his brother had preached it without knowing that the Shepherds were in existence, for he had only come late the night before, and there was so much to say about their home, that the younger brother had not said a word about his parish before church, though the Kings and their guests were very near his heart.

But it was of no use to say so. It was the *truth* that wounded the farmer and his wife, and no one could make that otherwise. They did not choose to hear their sin rebuked, so they made an excuse by pretending to take offence, and except when they now and then went to the next parish to a meeting-house, cut themselves off from all that might disturb them in the sole pursuit of gain. It is awful to think of such hardening of the heart, first towards man, then towards the warnings of God.

And mind, whoever chooses profit rather than mercy, is in the path of Farmer Shepherd.

Some certainty as to Lady Jane Selby's feelings came on the second evening of Paul's illness. Mrs. Crabbe, the housekeeper, was seen with infinite trouble and disgust getting her large person over the stiles across the path fields. A call from her was almost a greater event than one from my Lady herself. Why! Mother had been her still-room maid, and always spoke to her as 'Ma'am,' and she called her 'Mary,' and she had chosen Matilda's name for her, and had given her a silver watch!

So when Mrs. Crabbe had found her way in, and had been set down to rest in the arm-chair, she proceeded to give 'Mary' a good round scolding against being weak and soft-hearted, saying at last that my Lady was quite in a way about it. She was sure that Harold would catch his death of cold, putting him to sleep in the kitchen, upon the stones—and so—my Lady had sent off the cart with the little chair-bed, that would take down and put up again—mattress, bed-clothes, and all.

That was a comfortable finish to the scolding! Not that it was a finish though, for the thanks made Mrs. Crabbe afraid the family thought themselves forgiven, so she went on to declare they all would be pinched, and get into debt, and she should advise her god-daughter, Matilda, not to help them with a farthing of her wages, and as to going without their full meals, that was what none of them were fit to do. With which it appeared that the cart was bringing a can of broth, a couple of rabbits, some calves'-feet jelly, and a bottle of port wine for Alfred, who lived on that and cod-liver oil more than on any other nourishment.

At that rate, Lady Jane's displeasure did not seem likely to do much harm; but there was pain in it too, for when Mrs. Crabbe had managed to get up-stairs, past the patch-work quilt that was hung up to shelter Paul from the draught, and had seen Alfred, and been shocked to find how much wasted he was since she last had seen him, she said, 'One thing you know—my Lady says she can't have Miss Selby coming down here to see Alfred while this great lad is always about. And I'm sure it is not proper for her at any time, such a young lady as she is, over all those inconvenient stiles. I declare I shall speak to Mr. Price about them.'

Losing Miss Jane's visits was to Alfred like losing a sunbeam, and his spirit felt very dreary after he had heard this sentence. Ellen knew her well enough to suspect that she was very sorry, but that she could not help herself; and Mrs. King caught the brother and sister making such grumbling speeches to each other about the old lady's crossness, that her faithful, grateful spirit was quite grieved, and she spoke strongly up for the just, right-minded lady to whom she had loyally looked up for many and many a year, though, with the right sort of independence, she would not give up to any one's opinion what she knew to be her duty.

'We all knew it must cost us something,' she said, 'and we'll try to be ready with it, though it does go to one's heart that the first should be what vexes you, my Alfy; but it won't be for long.'

'No, Mother; but if it ain't here long? Oh! I don't seem to have nothing to look to if Miss Jane ain't coming here no more, with her pretty ways!'

And there were large tears on his cheeks. Mrs. King had tears in her eyes too, but she bent down over the boy, and turning his eyes to the little picture on the wall, she said in a whisper in his ear, 'Didn't He bear His Cross for the sake of other people?' Alfred did not answer; he turned his face in towards the pillow, and though Ellen thought he was crying, it did not seem to her to be so sadly.

Cost them something their kindness did. To be sure, there came a party of boys with the master from Ragglesford, when there had been time for them to write the history of the robbery to their homes; and as it came just before the monthly letter which they all had to write by way of practice, to be shewn up to the master, it was a real treasure to them to have such a story to tell. Some of their friends, especially the uncle who gave the watch, had sent small sums of money for the lad who had behaved so well, and these altogether came to a fair amount, which the boys were highly pleased to give over into Mrs. King's hands. She, like Harold, never made the smallest question that it was all for Paul's benefit, and though, when she mentioned it to him, he gave a cheery smile, and said it would lessen the cost of his illness to her, yet she put it all aside with the first twelve-and-sixpence. She told Ellen that it went against her to touch the orphan's money, and that unless it came to very bad times indeed, it should be kept to set him up decently when he should recover.

No one else could afford aid in money, not Mr. Cope, for he had little more than a maintenance for himself; indeed, Mrs. King was not in a station where it would seem becoming to offer alms to her. Lady Jane gave help in nourishing food, but the days when this would come were uncertain, and she had made a resolution against undertaking any share of the expense, lest she should seem to encourage Mary King, as she said, in such weak good nature —cramming up her house with a strange boy like that, when she had quite enough to do with her own son. So they had to fight on as they could; and the first week, when Paul's illness was at the height, Ellen had so much more to do for Alfred and about the house, and was so continually called off her work, that she could not finish Mrs. Crabbe's gown as soon as was expected; and the ladies' maid, who was kept waiting, took huff, and sent her new purple silk to Elbury to be madeup.

It is not quite certain that Ellen did not shed a few tears.

Harold had to go without his butter, and once took it much to heart that his mother would buy no shrimps for tea, but after some one had whispered to him that if there were a trouble about rent, or about Mr. Blunt's bill, Peggy would be sold, he bore it all pretty well; and after all, Alfred and Paul were so apt to give him tastes of their dainties, that he had not much loss!

Rent was the care. The pig was killed and cut up to great advantage; Mrs. King sold a side of it at once, which went a good way towards it, but not the whole; and there was a bad debt of John Farden's for bread, contracted last winter, and which he had never paid off in the summer. That would just have made it up, but what hopes were there of that?

Just then, however, came a parcel from Matilda. It was her way of helping her family to send them the clothes which her mistresses allowed her to have when they left them off, when Mrs. King either made them up for herself or Ellen, or disposed of them at Elbury.

What a treat those parcels were! How curious were all the party at the unpacking, looking at the many odd things that were sure to come out, on the happy doubtful certainty that each one would be remembered by the good sister.

So there were the little directed parcels—a neat knitted grey and black handkerchief for Mother to wear in the shop; a whole roll of fashion-books for Ellen, and a nice little pocket-book besides; and a bundle of 'Illustrated News' to amuse the boys; a precious little square book of 'Hymns for the Sick' for Alfred; and a famous pair of riding-gloves, like bears' paws, for Harold. And what rolls besides! Worn flimsy dresses, once pretty, but now only fit for the old-clothes man, yet whose trimmings Ellen pulled out and studied; bonnets that looked as if they had been sat upon; rolls of soft ragged cambric handkerchiefs, on which Mrs. King seized as the most valuable part of the cargo, so useful would they be to poor Alfred; some few real good things, in especial, a beautiful thick silk dress which had been stained, but which dyeing would render very useful; and a particularly nice grey cloth mantle, which Matilda had mentioned in her letter as likely to be useful to Ellen—it was not at all the worse for wear, except as to the lining of the hood, and she should just fancy Ellen in it.

Ellen could just fancy herself in it. She had a black silk one, which had come in the same way, and looked very well, but it was just turning off, and it was not warm enough for winter without a shawl under it. That grey looked as if it was made for her, it suited her shoulders and her shape so well! She put it on and twisted about in it, and then she saw her good mother not saying one word, and knew she was thinking of the sum that was wanting to the rent.

'Well, Mother,' said Ellen, 'I'll go in and take the things to Betsey on the next market-day, and if we can get thirty shillings on them without the mantle—'

'Yes, if you can, my dear,' said her mother; 'I'm sure I should be very glad for you to have it, but you see—'

And Mrs. King sighed.

Ellen passed by Paul on the landing, and saw him with his face flushed with pain and fever, trying to smile at her. She remembered how her unkind words had brought trouble on him, and how her mother had begun by telling her that they must give up their own wishes if they were to nurse him.

Ellen went to Elbury on the market-day, and by the help of Betsey Hardman, she got great credit for her bargaining. She brought home thirty shillings, and ten shillings' worth of soap for the shop, where that article was running low; but she did not bring home the cloak, though Betsey had told her a silk cloak over a shawl looked so mean! and she feared all the servants at the Grange would think the same!

'They always were good children to me,' said Mrs. King to Mr. Cope, 'but somehow, since Paul has been here, I think they are better than ever! There's poor Alfred, though his cough has been so bad of late, has been so thoughtful and so good; he says he's quite ashamed to find how patient Paul is under so much sharper pain than he ever had, and he's ready to send anything to Paul that he fancies will do him good—quite carried out of himself, you see; and there's Harold, so much steadier; I've hardly had to find fault with him since that poor boy made off—he's sure to come in in time, and takes care not to disturb his brother, and helps his sister and me all he can.'

Mr. Cope was not at all surprised that the work of mercy was blessed to all the little household, nor that it drew out all the better side of their dispositions.

There was no positive change, nor sudden resolution, to alter Harold; but he had been a good deal startled by Dick's wickedness, and in him had lost a tempter. Besides, he considered Paul as his own friend, received for his sake, and therefore felt himself bound to do all he could for him, and though he was no nurse, he could do much to set his mother and Ellen free to attend to their patients. And Paul's illness, though so much less dangerous, frightened and subdued Harold much more than the quiet gradual pining away of Alfred, to which he was used. The severe pain, the raging fever, and the ramblings in talk, were much more fearful things to witness than the low cough, the wearing sore, and the helpless languor, though there was much hope for the one, and scarcely any for the other. While to Harold's apprehension, Alfred was always just the same, only worsening visibly from month to month; Paul was better or worse every time he came in, and when fresh from hearing his breath gasp with sharp pain, or receiving his feeble thanks for some slight service, it was not in Harold to go out and get into thoughtless mischief.

Moreover, there were helpful things to do at home, such as Harold liked. He was fond of chopping wood, so he was very obliging about the oven, and what he liked best of all was helping his mother in certain evening cookeries of sweet-meats, by receipts from Mrs. Crabbe. On the day of the expedition from Ragglesford, the young gentlemen had found out that Mrs. King's bottles contained what they called 'the real article and no mistake,' much better than what the old woman at the turnpike sold; and so they were, for

Mrs. King made them herself, and, like an honest woman, without a morsel of sham in them. She was not going to break the Eighth Commandment by cheating in a comfit any more than by stealing a purse; and the children of Friarswood had long known that, and bought all the 'lollies' that they were not naughty enough to buy on Sundays, when, as may be supposed, her shutters were not shut only for a decent show.

And now Harold did not often ride up to the school without some little master giving him a commission for some variety of sweet-stuff; and though Mrs. King used to say it was a pity the children should throw away their money in that fashion, it brought a good deal into her till, and Harold greatly liked assisting at the manufacture. How often he licked his fingers during the process need not be mentioned; but his objection to Ragglesford was quite gone off, now that some one was nearly certain to be looking out for him, with a good-natured greeting, or an inquiry for Paul. He knew one little boy from another, and felt friendly with them all, and he really was quite grieved when the holidays came, and they wished him good-bye. The coach that had been hired to take them to Elbury seemed something to watch for now, and some thoughtful boy stopped all the whooping and hurraing as they came near the house on the bridge. Some other stopped the coach, and they all came dropping off it like a swarm of black flies, and tumbling into the shop, where Mrs. King and her daughter had need to have had a dozen pair of hands to have served them, and they did not go till they had cleared out her entire stock of sweet things and gingerbread; nay, some of them would have gone off without their change, if she had not raced out to catch them with it after they were climbing up the coach, and then the silly fellows said they hated coppers! And meeting Harold and his post-bag on his way home from Elbury, they raised such a tremendous cheer at him that poor Peggy seemed to make but three springs from the milestone to the bridge, and he could not so much as touch his cap by way of answer.

Somehow, even after those droll customers were gone, every Saturday's reckoning was a satisfactory one. More always seemed to come in than went out. The potatoes had been unusually free from disease in Mrs. King's garden, and every one came for them; the second pig turned out well; a lodger at the butcher's took a fancy to her buns; and on the whole, winter, when her receipts were generally at the lowest, was now quite a prosperous time with her. The great pressure and near anxiety she had expected had not come, and something was being put by every week towards the bill for flour, and for Mr. Blunt's account, so that she began to hope that after all the Savings Bank would not have to be left quite bare.

Quite unexpectedly, John Farden came in for a share of the savings of an old aunt at service, and, like an honest fellow as he was, he got himself out of debt at once. This quite settled all Mrs. King's fears; Mr. Blunt and the miller would both have their due, and she really believed she should be no poorer!

Then she recollected the widow's cruse of oil, and tears of thankfulness and faith came into her eyes, and other tears dropped when she remembered the other more precious comfort that the stranger had brought into the widow's house, but she knew that the days of miracles and cures past hope were gone, and that the Christian woman's promise was 'that her children should come again,' but not till the resurrection of the just.

And though to her eye each frost was freshly piercing her boy's breast, each warm damp day he faded into greater feebleness, yet the hope was far clearer. He was happy and content. He had laid hold of the blessed hope of Everlasting Life, and was learning to believe that the Cross laid on him here was in mercy to make him fit for Heaven, first making him afraid and sorry for his sins, and ready to turn to Him Who could take them away, and then almost becoming gladness, in the thought of following his Master, though so far off.

Not that Alfred often said such things, but they breathed peace over his mind, and made Scripture-reading, prayers, and hymns very delightful to him, especially those in Matilda's book; and he dwelt more than he told any one on Mr. Cope's promise, when he trusted to be made more fully 'one with Christ' in the partaking of His Cup of Life. It used to be his treat, when no one was looking, to read over that Service in his Prayer-book, and to think of the time. It was like a kind of step; he could fix his mind on that, and the sense of forgiveness he hoped for therein, better than on the great change that was coming; when there was much fear and shrinking from the pain, and some dread of what as yet seemed strange and unknown, he thought he should feel lifted up so as to be able to bear the thought, when that holy Feast should have come to him.

All this made him much less occupied with himself, and he took much more share in what was going on; he could be amused and playful, cared for all that Ellen and Harold did, and was inclined to make the most of his time with his brother. It was like old happy times, now that Alfred had ceased to be fretful, and Harold took heed not to distress him.

One thing to which Alfred looked forward greatly, was Paul's being able to come into his room, and the two on their opposite sides of the wall made many pleasant schemes for the talk and reading that were to go on. But when the day came, Alfred was more disappointed than pleased.

Paul had been cased, by Lady Jane's orders, in flannel; he had over that a pair of trousers of Alfred's—much too long, for the Kings were very tall, and he was small and stunted in growth—and a great wrapping-gown that Mr. Cope had once worn when he was ill at college, and over his shaven head a night-cap that had been their father's.

Ellen, with many directions from Alfred, had made him up a couch with three chairs, and the cushions Alfred used to have when he could leave his bed; the fire was made up brightly, and Mrs. King and Harold helped Paul into the room.

But all the rheumatic pain was by no means over, and walking made him feel it; he was dreadfully weak, and was so giddy and faint after the first few steps, that they could not bring him to shake hands with Alfred as both had wished, but had to lay him down as fast as they could. So tired was he, that he could hardly say anything all the time he was there; and Alfred had to keep silence for fear of wearying him still more. There was a sort of shyness, too, which hindered the two from even letting their eyes meet, often as they had heard each other's voices, and had greeted one another through the thin partition. As Paul lay with his eyes shut, Alfred raised himself to take a good survey of the sharp pinched features, the hollow cheeks, deep-sunk pits for the eyes,—and yellow ghastly skin of the worn face, and the figure, so small and wasted that it was like nothing, curled up in all those wraps. One who could read faces better than young Alfred could, would have gathered not only that the boy who lay there had gone through a great deal, but that there was much mind and thought crushed down by misery, and a gentle nature not fit to stand up alone against it, and so sinking down without exertion.

And when Alfred was learning a verse of his favourite hymn—

'There is a rill whose waters rise—'

Paul's eye-lids rose, and looked him all over dreamily, comparing him perhaps with the notions he had carried away from his two former glimpses. Alfred did not look now so utterly different from anything he had seen before, since Mrs. King and Ellen had been hovering round his bed for nearly a month past; but still the fair skin, pink colour, dark eye-lashes, glossy hair, and white hands, were like a dream to him, as if they belonged to the pure land whither Alfred was going, and he was quite loath to hear him speak like another boy, as he knew he could do, having often listened to his talk through the wall. At the least sign of Alfred's looking up, he turned away his eyes as if he had been doing something by stealth.

He came in continually after this; and little things each day, and Harold's talk, made the two acquainted and like boys together; but it was not till Christmas

Day that they felt like knowing each other.

It was the first time Paul felt himself able to be of any use, for he was to be left in charge of Alfred, while Mrs. King and both her other children went to church. Paul was sadly crippled still, and every frost filled his bones with acute pain, and bent him like an old man, so that he was still a long way from getting down-stairs, but he could make a shift to get about the room, and he looked greatly pleased when Alfred declared that he should want nobody else to stay with him in the morning.

Very glad he was that his mother would not be kept from Ellen's first Holy Communion. Owing to the Curate not being a priest, the Feast had not been celebrated since Michaelmas; but a clergyman had come to help Mr. Cope, that the parish might not be deprived of the Festival on such a day as Christmas.

Harold, though in a much better mood than at the Confirmation time, was not as much concerned to miss it as perhaps he ought to have been. Thought had not come to him yet, and his head was full of the dinner with the servants at the Grange. It was sad that he and Ellen should alone be able to go to it; but it would be famous for all that! Ay, and so were the young postman's Christmas-boxes!

So Paul and Alfred were left together, and held their tongues for full five minutes, because both felt so odd. Then Alfred said something about reading the Service, and Paul offered to read it to him.

Paul had not only been very well taught, but had a certain gift, such as not many people have, for reading aloud well. Alfred listened to those Psalms and Lessons as if they had quite a new meaning in them, for the right sound and stress on the right words made them sound quite like another thing; and so Alfred said when he left off.

'I'm sure they do to me,' said Paul. 'I didn't know much about "good-will to men" last Christmas.'

'You've not had overmuch good-will from them, neither,' said Alfred, 'since you came out.'

'What! not since I've been at Friarswood?' exclaimed Paul. 'Why, I used to think all *that* was only something in a book.'

'All what?' asked Alfred.

'All about—why, loving one's neighbour—and the Good Samaritan, and so on. I never saw any one do it, you know, but it was comfortable like to read about it; and when I watched to your mother and all of you, I saw how it was

127

about one's neighbour; and then, what with that and Mr. Cope's teaching, I got to feel how it was—about God!' and Paul's face looked very grave and peaceful.

'Well,' said Alfred, 'I don't know as I ever cared about it much—not since I was a little boy. It was the fun last Christmas.'

And Paul looking curious, Alfred told all about the going out for holly, and the dining at the Grange, and the snap-dragon over the pudding, till he grew so eager and animated that he lost breath, and his painful cough came on, so that he could just whisper, 'What did you do?'

'Oh! I don't know. We had prayers, and there was roast beef for dinner, but they gave it to me where it was raw, and I couldn't eat it. Those that had friends went out; but 'twasn't much unlike other days.'

'Poor Paul!' sighed Alfred.

'It won't be like that again, though,' said Paul, 'even if I was in a Union. I know—what I know now.'

'And, Paul,' said Alfred, after a pause, 'there's one thing I should like if I was you. You know our Blessed Saviour had no house over Him, but was left out of the inn, and nobody cared for Him.'

Paul did not make any answer; and Alfred blushed all over.

Presently Alfred said, 'Harold will run in soon. I say, Paul, would you mind reading me what they will say after the Holy Sacrament—what the Angels sang is the beginning.'

Paul found it, and felt as if he must stand to read such praise.

'Thank you,' said Alfred. 'I'm glad Mother and Ellen are there. They'll remember us, you know. Did you hear what Mr. Cope promised me?'

Paul had not heard; and Alfred told him, adding, 'It will be the Ember-week in Lent. You'll be one with me then, Paul?'

'I'd like to promise,' said Paul fervently; 'but you see, when I'm well—'

'Oh, you won't go away for good. My Lady, or Mr. Cope, will get you work; and I want you to be Mother's good son instead of me; and a brother to Harold and Ellen.'

'I'd never go if I could help it,' said Paul; 'I sometimes wish I'd never got better! I wish I could change with you, Alfred; nobody would care if 'twas me; nor I'm sure I shouldn't.'

'I should like to get well!' said Alfred slowly, and sighing. 'But then you've been a much better lad than I was.'

'I don't know why you should say that,' said Paul, with his hand under his chin, rather moodily. 'But if I thought I could be good and go on well, I would not mind so much. I say, Alfred, when people round go on being—like Tom Boldre, you know—do you think one can always feel that about God being one's Father, and church home, and all the rest?'

'I can't say—I never tried,' said Alfred. 'But you know you can always go to church—and then the Psalms and Lessons tell you those things. Well, and you can go to the Holy Sacrament—I say, Paul, if you take it the first time with me, you'll always remember me again every time after.'

'I must be very odd ever to forget you!' said Paul, not far from crying. 'Ha!' he exclaimed, 'they are coming out of church!'

'I want to say one thing more, while I've got it in my head,' said Alfred. 'Mr. Cope said all this sickness was a cross to me, and I'd got to take it up for our Saviour's sake. Well, and then mayn't yours be being plagued and bullied, without any friends? I'm sure something like it happened to our Lord; and He never said one word against them. Isn't that the way you may be to follow Him?'

Illness and thought had made such things fully plain to Alfred, and his words sank deep into Paul's mind; but there was not time for any answer, for Harold was heard unlocking the door, and striding up three steps at a time, sending his voice before him. 'Well, old chaps, have you quarrelled yet? Have you been jolly together? I say, Mrs. Crabbe told Ellen that the pudding was put into the boiler at eight o'clock last night; and my Lady and Miss Jane went in to give it a stir! I'm to bring you home a slice, you know; and Paul will know what a real pudding is like.'

The two boys spent a happy quiet afternoon with Mrs. King; and Charles Hayward brought all the singing boys down, that they might hear the carols outside the window. Paul, much tired, was in his bed by that time; but his last thought was that 'Good-will to Men' had come home to him at last.

CHAPTER XI—BETTER DAYS FOR PAUL

Paul's reading was a great prize to Alfred, for he soon grew tired himself; his sister could not spare time to read to him, and if she did, she went mumbling on like a bee in a bottle. Her mother did much the same, and Harold used to stumble and gabble, so that it was horrible to hear him. Such reading as Paul's was a new light to them all, and was a treat to Ellen as she worked as much as to Alfred; and Paul, with hands as clean as Alfred's, was only too happy to get hold of a book, and infinitely enjoyed the constant supply kept up by Miss Selby, to make up for her not coming herself.

Then came the making out the accounts, a matter dreaded by all the family. Ellen and Alfred both used to do the sums; but as they never made them the same, Mrs. King always went by some reckoning of her own by pencil dots on her thumb-nail, which took an enormous time, but never went wrong. So the slate and the books came up after tea, one night, and Ellen set to work with her mother to pick out every one's bill. There might be about eight customers who had Christmas bills; but many an accountant in a London shop would think eight hundred a less tough business than did the King family these eight; especially as there was a debtor and creditor account with four, and coals, butcher's meat, and shoes for man and horse, had to be set against bread, tea, candles, and the like.

One pound of tea, 3s. 6d., that was all very well; but an ounce and a half of the same made Ellen groan, and look wildly at the corner over Alfred's bed, as if in hopes she should there see how to set it down, so as to work it.

'Fourpence, all but—' said a voice from the arm-chair by the fire.

Ellen did not take any particular heed, but announced the fact that three shillings were thirty-six pence, and six was forty-two. Also that sixteen ounces were one pound, and sixteen drams one ounce; but there she got stuck, and began making figures and rubbing them out, as if in hopes that would clear up her mind. Mrs. King pecked on for ten minutes on her nail.

'Well,' she said, 'Paul's right; it is fourpence.'

'However did you do it?' asked Ellen.

'As 16 to 1.5, so 42,' quoth Paul quickly. 'Three halves into 42; 21 and 42 is 63; 63 by 16, gives 3 and fifteen-sixteenths. You can't deduct a sixteenth of a penny, so call it fourpence.'

Ellen and Alfred were as wise as to the working as they were before.

Next question—Paul's answer came like the next line in the book—Mrs. King proved him right, and so on till she was quite tired of the proofs, and began to trust him. Alfred asked how he could possibly do such things, which seemed to him a perfect riddle.

'I should have had my ears pretty nigh pulled off if I took five minutes to work *that* in my head,' said Paul. 'But I've forgotten things now; I could do it faster once.'

'I'm sure you hadn't need,' said Mrs. King; 'it's enough to distract one's senses to count so fast. All in your poor head too!'

'And I've got to write them all out to-morrow,' said Ellen dismally; 'I must wait till dark, or I shan't set a stitch of work. I wish people would pay ready money, and then one wouldn't have to set down their bills. Here's Mr. Cope, bread—bread—bread, as long as my arm!'

'If you didn't mind, maybe I could save you the trouble, Miss Ellen,' said Paul.

'Did you ever make out a bill?' asked Mrs. King.

'Never a real one; but every Thursday I used to do sham ones. Once I did a jeweller's bill for twelve thousand pounds and odd! It is so long since I touched a pen, that may be I can't write; but I should like to try.'

Ellen brought a pen, and the cover of a letter; and hobbling up to the table, he took the pen, cleared it of a hair that was sticking in it, made a scratch or two weakly and ineffectually, then wrote in a neat clear hand, without running up or down, 'Friarswood, Christmas.'

'A pretty hand as ever I saw!' said Mrs. King. 'Well, if you can write like that, and can be trusted to make no mistakes, you might write out our bills; and we'd be obliged to you most kindly.'

And so Paul did, so neatly, that when the next evening Mr. Cope walked in with the money, he said, looking at Harold, 'Ah! my ancient Saxon, I must make my compliments to you: I did not think you could write letters as well as you can carry them.'

''Twas Paul did it, Sir,' said Harold.

'Yes, Sir; 'twas Paul,' said Mrs. King. 'The lad is a wonderful scholar: he told off all the sums as if they was in print; and to hear him read—'tis like nothing I ever heard since poor Mrs. Selby, Miss Jane's mother.'

'I saw he had been very well instructed—in acquaintance with the Bible, and the like.'

'And, Sir, before I got to know him for a boy that would not give a false account of himself, I used to wonder whether he could have run away from some school, and have friends above the common. If you observe, Sir, he speaks so remarkably well.'

Mr. Cope had observed it. Paul spoke much better English than did even the Kings; though Ellen was by way of being very particular, and sometimes a little mincing.

'You are quite sure it is not so?' he said, a little startled at Mrs. King's surmise.

'Quite sure now, Sir. I don't believe he would tell a falsehood on no account; and besides, poor lad!' and she smiled as the tears came into her eyes, 'he's so taken to me, he wouldn't keep nothing back from me, no more than my own boys.'

'I'm sure he ought not, Mrs. King,' said the Curate, 'such a mother to him as you have been. I should like to examine him a little. With so much education, he might do something better for himself than field-labour.'

'A very good thing it would be, Sir,' said Mrs. King, looking much cheered; 'for I misdoubt me sometimes if he'll ever be strong enough to gain his bread that way—at least, not to be a good workman. There! he's not nigh so tall as Harold; and so slight and skinny as he is, going about all bent and slouching, even before his illness! Why, he says what made him stay so long in the Union was that he looked so small and young, that none of the farmers at Upperscote would take him from it; and so at last he had to go on the tramp.'

Mr. Cope went up-stairs, and found Ellen, as usual, at her needle, and Paul in the arm-chair close by Alfred, both busied in choosing and cutting out pictures from Matilda's 'Illustrated News,' with which Harold ornamented the wall of the stair-case and landing. Mr. Cope sat down, and made them laugh with something droll about the figures that were lying spread on Alfred.

'So, Paul,' he said, 'I find Mrs. King has engaged you for her accountant.'

'I wish I could do anything to be of any use,' said Paul.

'I've half a mind to ask you some questions in arithmetic,' said Mr. Cope, with his merry eyes upon the boy, and his mouth looking grave; 'only I'm afraid you might puzzle me.'

'I can't do as I used, Sir,' said Paul, rather nervously; 'I've forgotten ever so much; and my head swims.'

The slate was lying near; Mr. Cope pushed it towards him, and said, 'Well, will you mind letting me see how you can write from dictation?'

And taking up one of the papers, he read slowly several sentences from a description of a great fire, with some tolerably long-winded newspaper words in them. When he paused, and asked for the slate, there it all stood, perfectly spelt, well written, and with all the stops and capitals in the right places.

'Famously done, Paul! Well, and do you know where this place was?' naming the town.

Paul turned his eyes about for a moment, and then gave the name of a county.

'That'll do, Paul. Which part of England?'

'Midland.'

And so on, Mr. Cope got him out of his depth by asking about the rivers, and made him frown and look teased by a question about a battle fought in that county. If he had ever known, he had forgotten, and he was weak and easily confused; but Mr. Cope saw that he had read some history and learnt some geography, and was not like some of the village boys, who used to think Harold had been called after Herod—a nice namesake, truly!

'Who taught you all this, Paul?' he said. 'You must have had a cleverer master than is common in Unions. Who was he?'

'He was a Mr. Alcock, Sir. He was a clever man. They said in the House that he had been a bit of a gentleman, a lawyer, or a clerk, or something, but that he could never keep from the bottle.'

'What! and so they keep him for a school-master?'

'He was brought in, Sir; he'd got that mad fit that comes of drink, Sir, and was fresh out of gaol for debt. And when he came to, he said he'd keep the school for less than our master that was gone. He couldn't do anything else, you see.'

'And how did he teach you?'

'He knocked us about,' said Paul, drawing his shoulders together with an unpleasant recollection; 'he wasn't so bad to me, because I liked getting my tasks, and when he was in a good humour, he'd say I was a credit to him, and order me in to read to him in the evening.'

'And when he was not?'

'That was when he'd been out. They said he'd been at the gin-shop; but he used to be downright savage,' said Paul. 'At last he never thought it worth while to teach any lessons but mine, and I used to hear the other classes; but the inspector came all on a sudden, and found it out one day when he'd hit a little lad so that his nose was bleeding, and so he was sent off.'

'How long ago was this?'

'Going on for a year,' said Paul.

'Didn't the inspector want you to go to a training-school?' said Alfred.

'Yes; but the Guardians wouldn't hear of it.'

'Did you wish it?' asked Mr. Cope.

'I liked my liberty, Sir,' was the answer; and Paul looked down.

'Well, and what you do think now you've tried your liberty?'

Paul didn't make any answer, but finding that good-humoured face still waiting, he said slowly, 'Why, Sir, it was well-nigh the worst of all to find I was getting as stupid as the cows.'

Mr. Cope laughed, but not so as to vex him; and added, 'So that was the way you learnt to be a reader, Paul. Can you tell me what books you used to read to this master?'

Paul paused; and Alfred said, '"Uncle Tom's Cabin," Sir; he told us the story of that.'

'Yes,' said Paul; 'but that wasn't all: there was a book about Paris, and all the people in the back lanes there; and a German prince who came, and was kind.'

'You must not tell them stories out of that book, Paul,' said Mr. Cope quickly, for he knew it was a very bad one.

'No, Sir,' said Paul; 'but most times it was books he called philosophy, that I couldn't make anything of—no story, and all dull; but he was very savage if I got to sleep over them, till I hated the sight of them.'

'I'm glad you did, my poor boy,' said Mr. Cope. 'But one thing more. Tell me how, with such a man as this, you could have learnt about the Bible and Catechism, as you have done.'

'Oh,' said Paul, 'we had only the Bible and Testament to read in the school, because they were the cheapest; and the chaplain asked us about the Catechism every Sunday.'

'What was the chaplain's name?'

Paul was able, with some recollection, to answer; but he knew little about the clergyman, who was much overworked, and seldom able to give any time to the paupers.

Three days after, Mr. Cope again came into the post-office.

'Well, Mrs. King, I suppose you don't need to be told that our friend Paul has spoken nothing but truth. The chaplain sends me his baptismal registry, for which I asked. Just seventeen he must be—a foundling, picked up at about three weeks old, January 25th, 1836. They fancy he was left by some tramping musicians, but never were able to trace them—at least, so the chaplain hears from some of the people who remember it. Being so stunted, and looking younger than he is, no farmer would take him from the House, and the school-master made him useful, so he was kept on till the grand exposure that he told us of.'

'Ah! Sir,' said Mrs. King,' I'm afraid that master was a bad man. I only wonder the poor lad learnt no more harm from him!'

'One trembles to think of the danger,' said Mr. Cope; 'but you see there's often a guard over those who don't seek the temptation, and perhaps this poor fellow's utter ignorance of anything beyond the Union walls helped him to let the mischief pass by his understanding, better than if he had had any experience of the world.'

'I doubt if he'll ever have that, Sir,' said Mrs. King, her sensible face lighting up rather drolly; 'there's Harold always laughing at him for being so innocent, and yet so clever at his book.'

'So much the better for him,' said Mr. Cope. 'The Son of Sirach never said a wiser word than that "the knowledge of wickedness is not wisdom." Why, Mrs. King, what have I said? you look as if you had a great mind to laugh at me.'

'I beg your pardon, Sir,' said Mrs. King, much disconcerted at what seemed to her as if it might have been disrespect, though that was only Mr. Cope's droll way of putting it, 'I never meant—'

'Well, but what were you thinking of?'

'Why, Sir, I beg your pardon, but I was thinking it wouldn't have been amiss if he had had sense enough to keep himself clean and tidy.'

'I agree with you,' said Mr. Cope, laughing, and seeing she used 'innocent' in a slightly different sense from what he did; 'but perhaps Union cleanliness was not inviting, and he'd not had you to bring him up to fresh cheeks like Harold's. Besides, I believe it was half depression and want of heart to exert himself, when there was no one to care for him; and he certainly had not been taught either self-respect, or to think cleanliness next to godliness.'

'Poor lad—no,' said Mrs. King; 'nor I don't think he'd do it again, and I trust he'll never be so lost again.'

'Lost, and found,' said Mr. Cope gravely. 'Another thing I was going to say was, that this irreverent economy of the Guardians, in allowing no lesson-books but the Bible, seems to have, after all, been blest to him in his knowledge of it, like an antidote to the evil the master poured in.'

'Yes, Sir,' said Mrs. King, 'just so; only he says, that though he liked it, because, poor lad, there was nothing else that seemed to him to speak kind or soft, he never knew how much it was meant for him, nor it didn't seem to touch him home till he came to you, Sir.'

Mr. Cope half turned away. His bright eyes had something very like a tear in them, for hardly anything could have been said to make the young clergyman so happy, as to tell him that any work of his should be blessed; but he went on talking quickly, to say that the chaplain gave a still worse account of Alcock than Paul's had been, saying that some gentlemen who had newly become Guardians at the time of the inspector's visit, had taken up the matter, and had been perfectly shocked at the discoveries they had made about the man to whom the poor children had been entrusted.

On his dismissal, some of the old set, who were all for cheapness, had talked of letting young Blackthorn act as school-master; but as he was so very young, and had been brought up by this wretched man, the gentlemen would not hear of it; and as they could not afford to accept the inspector's offer of recommending him to a government school, he had been sent out in quest of employment, as being old enough to provide for himself. Things had since, the chaplain said, been put on a much better footing, and he himself had much more time to attend to the inmates. As to Paul, he was glad to hear that he was in good hands; he said he had always perceived him to be a very clever boy, and knew no harm of him but that he was a favourite with Alcock, which he owned had made him very glad to get him out of the House, lest he should carry on the mischief.

Mr. Cope and Mrs. King were both of one mind, that this was hard measure. So it was. Man's measure always is either over hard or over soft, because he cannot see all sides at once. Now they saw Paul's side, his simplicity, and his suffering; the chaplain had only seen the chances of his conveying the seeds of ungodly teaching to the workhouse children; he could not tell that the pitch which Paul had not touched by his own will, had not stuck by him—probably owing to that very simplicity which had made him so helpless in common life.

Having learnt all this, Mr. Cope proposed to Paul to use the time of his recovery in learning as much as he could, so as to be ready in case any opportunity should offer for gaining his livelihood by his head rather than by his hands.

Paul's face glowed. He liked nothing better than to be at a book, and with Mr. Cope to help him by bright encouragements and good-natured explanations instead of tweaks of the ears and raps on the knuckles, what could be pleasanter? So Mr. Cope lent him books, set him questions, and gave him pen, ink, and copy-book, and he toiled away with them till his senses grew dazed, and his back ached beyond bearing; so that 'Mother,' as he called her now, caught him up, and made him lie on his bed to rest, threatening to tell Mr. Cope not to set him anything so hard; while Ellen watched in wonder at any one being so clever, and was proud of whatever Mr. Cope said he did well; and Harold looked on him as a more extraordinary creature than the pie-bald horse in the show, who wore a hat and stood on his hind legs, since he really was vexed when book and slate were taken out of his hands.

He would have over-tasked himself in his weakness much more, if it had not been for his lovingness to Alfred. To please Alfred was always his first thought; and even if a difficult sum were just on the point of proving itself, he would leave off at the first moment of seeing Alfred look as if he wanted to be read to, and would miss all his calculations, to answer some question—who was going down the village, or what that noise could be.

Alfred tried to be considerate, and was sorry when he saw by a furrow on Paul's brow that he was trying to win up again all that some trifling saying had made him lose. But Alfred was not scholar enough to perceive the teasing of such interruptions, and even had he been aware of it, he was not in a state when he could lie quite still long together without disturbing any one; he could amuse himself much less than formerly, and often had most distressing restless fits, when one or other of them had to give him their whole attention; and it was all his most earnest efforts could do to keep from the old habit of fretfulness and murmuring. And he grieved so much over the least want of temper, and begged pardon so earnestly for the least impatient word —even if there had been real provocation for it—that it was a change indeed since the time when he thought grumbling and complaint his privilege and relief. Nothing helped him more than Paul's reading Psalms to him—the 121st was his favourite—or saying over hymns to him in that very sweet voice so full of meaning. Sometimes Ellen and Paul would sing together, as she sat at her work, and it almost always soothed him to hear the Psalm tunes, that were like an echo from the church, about which he had cared so little when he had been able to go there in health and strength, but for which he now had such a longing! He came to be so used to depend on their singing the Evening Hymn to him, that one of the times when it was most hard for him to be patient, was one cold evening, when Ellen was so hoarse that she could not speak, and an unlucky draught in from the shop door had so knit Paul up again, that he was lying in his bed, much nearer screaming than singing.

Most of all, however, was Alfred helped by Mr. Cope's visits, and the looking forward to the promised Feast, with more earnestness as the time drew on, and he felt his own weakness more longing for the support and blessing of uniting his suffering with that of his Lord. 'In all our afflictions He was afflicted,' was a sound that came most cheeringly to him, and seemed to give him greater strength and good-will to bear his load of weakness.

There was a book which young Mrs. Selby had given his mother, which was often lying on his bed, and had marks in it at all the favourite places. Some he liked to look at himself, some for Paul to read to him. They were such sentences as these:

'My son, I descended from Heaven for thy salvation; I took upon Me thy miseries; not necessity, but charity, drawing Me thereto, that thou thyself mightest learn patience, and bear temporal miseries without grudging.'

'For from the hour of My Birth, even until My Death on the Cross, I was not without suffering and grief.'

And then again:

'Offer up thyself unto Me, and give thyself wholly for God, and thy offering shall be acceptable.'

'Behold, I offered up Myself wholly unto My Father for thee, and gave My whole Body and Blood for thy food, that I might be wholly thine, and that thou mightest continue Mine unto the end.'

So he might think of all that he went through as capable of being made a free offering, which God would accept for the sake of the One Great Offering, 'consuming and burning away' (as the book said) 'all his sins with the fire of Christ's love, and cleansing his conscience from all offences.' It was what he now felt in the words, 'Thy Will be done,' which he tried to say in full earnest; but he thought he should be very happy when he should go along with the offering ourselves, our souls, and bodies, to be a 'reasonable, holy, and lively sacrifice.'

Each of Mr. Cope's readings brought out or confirmed these refreshing hopes; and Paul likewise dwelt on such thoughts. Hardship had been a training to him, like sickness for Alfred; he knew what it was to be weary and heavy laden, and to want rest, and was ready to draw closer to the only Home and Father that he could claim. His gentle unresisting spirit was one that so readily forgot ill-will, that positively Harold cherished more dislike to the Shepherds than he did; and there was no struggle to forgive, no lack of charity for all men, so that hope and trust were free.

These two boys were a great deal to the young deacon. Perhaps he reckoned on his first ministration as a priest by Alfred's bedside, as much or even more than did the lad, for to him the whole household were as near and like-minded friends, though neither he nor they ever departed from the fitting manners of their respective stations. He was one who liked to share with others what was near his heart, and he had shewn Alfred the Service for the Ordination of Priests, and the Prayers for Grace that would be offered, and the holy vows that he would take upon him, and the words with which those great Powers would be conferred—those Powers that our Chief Shepherd left in trust for the pastors who feed His flock.

And once he had bent down and whispered to Alfred to pray that help might be given to him to use those powers faithfully.

So wore on the early spring; and the morning had come when he was to set out for the cathedral town, when Harold rode up to the parsonage door, and something in his looks as he passed the window made Mr. Cope hasten to the door to meet him.

'O Sir!' said Harold, bursting out crying as he began to speak, 'poor Alfred is took so bad; and Mother told me to tell you, Sir—if he's not better—he'll never live out the day!'

Poor Harold, who had never seemed to heed his brother's illness, was quite overwhelmed now. It had come upon him all at once.

'What is it? Has the doctor been?'

'No, Sir; I went in at six o'clock this morning to ask him to come out, and he said he'd come—and sent him a blister—but Alf was worse by the time I got back, Sir,—he can't breathe—and don't seem to notice.'

And without another word, nor waiting for comfort, Harold dug his heels into Peggy, passed his elbow over his eyes, and cantered on with the tears drying on his face in the brisk March wind.

There was no finishing breakfast for the Curate; he thrust his letters into his pocket, caught up his hat, and walked off with long strides for the post-office.

It shewed how different things were from usual, that Paul, who had hardly yet been four times down-stairs, his thin pointed face all in a flush, was the only person in the shop, trying with a very shaky hand to cut out some cheese for a great stout farm maid-servant, who evidently did not understand what was the matter, and stared doubly when the clergyman put his strong hand so as to steady Paul's trembling one, and gave his help to fold up the parcel.

'How is he, Paul?'

Paul was very near crying as he answered, 'Much worse, Sir. Mother has been up all night with him. O Sir! he did so want to live till you came home.'

'May I go up?' asked Mr. Cope.

Paul was sure that he might, and crept up after him. It was bad enough, but not quite so bad as Harold, in his fright, had made Mr. Cope believe. Poor boy! it had all come upon him now; and seeing his brother unable to speak and much oppressed, he fancied he did not know him, whereas Alfred was fully sensible, though too ill to do more than lift his eyes, and put out his weak fingers as Mr. Cope came into the room, where he was lying raised on his pillows, with his mother and sister doing all they could for him.

A terrible pain in the side had come on in the night, making every breath painful, every cough agonizing, and his whole face and brow were crimson with the effort of gasping.

Paul looked a moment but could not bear it, and went, and sat down on the top of the stairs; while Mr. Cope kindly held Alfred's hot hand, and Mrs. King, in her low patient tone, told how the attack had begun.

She was in the midst, when Mr. Blunt's gig was seen at the gate. His having thus hastened his coming was more than they had dared to hope; and while Mrs. King felt grateful for the kindness, Ellen feared that it shewed that he thought very badly of the case.

Mr. Cope was much hurried, but he could not bear to go till he had heard Mr. Blunt's opinion; so he went down to the kitchen, tried to console Paul by talking kindly to him, wrote a note, and read his letters.

They were much comforted to hear that Mr. Blunt thought that there was hope of subduing the present inflammatory pain; and though there was much immediate danger, it was not hastening so very fast to the end as they had at first supposed. Yet, in such a state as Alfred's, a few hours might finish all. There was no saying.

Already, when Mr. Cope went up again, the remedies had given some relief; and though the breaths came short and hard, like so many stabs, Alfred had put his head into an easier position, and his eyes and lips looked more free to look a greeting. There was so much wistful earnestness in his face, and it deeply grieved Mr. Cope to be forced to leave him, and in too much haste even to be able to pray with him.

'Well, Alfred, dear fellow,' he said, his voice trembling, 'I am come to wish you good-bye. I am comforted to find that Mr. Blunt thinks there is good hope that you will be here—that we shall be together when I come back. Yes, I know that is what is on your mind, and I do reckon most earnestly on it; but if it should not be His Will—here, Ellen, will you take care of this note? If he should be worse, will you send this to Mr. Carter, at Ragglesford? and I know he will come at once.'

The dew stood on Alfred's eye-lashes, and his lips worked. He looked up sadly to Mr. Cope, as if this did not answer his longings.

Mr. Cope replied to the look—'Yes, dear boy, but if it cannot be, still remember it is Communion. He can put us together. We all drink into one Spirit. I shall be engaged in a like manner—I would not—I could not go, Alfred, for pleasure—no, nor business—only for this. You must think that I am gone to bring you home the Gift—the greatest, best Gift—the one our Lord left with His disciples, to bear them through their sorrows and pains—through the light affliction that is but for a moment, but worketh an exceeding weight of glory. And if I should not be in time,' he added, nearly sobbing as he spoke, 'then—then, Alfred, the Gift, the blessing is yours all the same. It is the Great High Priest to Whom you must look—perhaps you may do so the more really if it should not be through—your friend. If we are disappointed, we will make a sacrifice of our disappointment. Good-bye, my boy; God bless you!' Bending close down to his face, he whispered, 'Think of me. Pray for me—now—always.' Then, rising hastily, he shook the hands of the mother and sister, ran down-stairs, and was gone.

CHAPTER XII—REST AT LAST

The east wind had been swept aside by gales from the warm south, and the spring was bursting out everywhere; the sky looked softly blue, instead of hard and chill; the sun made everything glisten: the hedges were full of catkins; white buds were on the purple twigs of the blackthorns; primroses were looking out on the sunny side of the road; the larks were mounting up, singing as if they were wild with delight; and the sunbeams were full of dancing gnats, as the Curate of Friarswood walked, with quick eager steps, towards the bridge.

His eyes were anxiously bent on the house, watching the white smoke rising from the chimney; then he hastened on to gain the first sight at the upper windows, feeling almost as he could have done had it been a brother who lay there; so much was his heart set on the first whom he had striven to help through the valley of the shadow of death. The window was open, but the blind was not drawn; and almost at the same moment the gate opened, some one looked out, and seeing him, waved his hand and arm in joyful signal towards some one within, and this gesture set Mr. Cope's heart at rest.

Was it Harold? No, it was Paul Blackthorn, who stood leaning on the wicket, as he held it open for the clergyman, at whom he looked up as if expecting some change, and a little surprised to find the same voice and manner.

'Well, Paul, then he is not worse?'

'No, Sir, thank you, he is better. The pain has left him, and he can speak again,' said Paul, but not very cheerfully.

'That is a great comfort! But who's that?' as a head, not Ellen's, appeared for a moment at the window.

'That's Miss King, Sir—Miss Matilda!'

'Oh! Well, and how are the bones, Paul? Better, I hope, since I see you are come out with the bees,' said Mr. Cope, laying his hand kindly on his shoulder (a thing fit to touch now, since it was in a fustian coat of poor Alfred's), and accommodating his swift strong steps to the feeble halt with which Paul still moved.

'Thank you, Sir, yes; I've been down here twice when the sun was out,' he said, as if it were a grand undertaking; but then, with a sudden smile, 'and poor Cæsar knew me, Sir; he came right across the road, and wagged his tail, and licked my hand.'

'Good old Cæsar! You were his best friend, Paul.—Well, Mrs. King, this is a blessing!'

Mrs. King looked sadly worn out with nursing, and her eyes were full of tears.

'Yes, Sir,' she said, 'indeed it is. My poor darling has been so much afraid he was too much set on your coming home, and yet so patient and quiet about it.'

'Then you ventured to wait?'

And Mr. Cope heard that the attack of inflammation had given way to remedies, but that Alfred was so much weakened, that they could not raise him again. He was sustained by as much nourishment as they could give him: but the disease had made great progress, and Mr. Blunt did not think that he could last many days. His eldest sister had come for a fortnight from her place, and was a great comfort to them all. 'And so is Paul,' said Mrs. King, looking for him kindly; 'I don't know what we should do without his help up-stairs and down. And, Sir, yesterday,' she added, colouring a good deal—'I beg your pardon, but I thought, maybe, you'd like to hear it—Alfred would have nobody else up with him in morning church-time—and made him read the most—of that Service, Sir.'

Mr. Cope's eyes glistened, and he said something huskily of being glad that Alfred could think of it.

It further appeared that Alfred had wished very much to see Miss Selby again, and that Mrs. King had sent the two sisters to the Grange to talk it over with Mrs. Crabbe, and word had been sent by Harold that morning that the young lady would come in the course of the afternoon.

Mr. Cope followed Mrs. King up-stairs; Alfred's face lighted up as his sister Matilda made way for the clergyman. He was very white, and his breath was oppressed; but his look had changed very much—it had a strange, still sort of brightness and peace about it. He spoke in very low tones, just above a whisper, and smiled as Mr. Cope took his hand, and spoke to him.

'Thank you, Sir. It is very nice,' he said.

'I thank God that He has let you wait for me,' said Mr. Cope.

'I am glad,' said Alfred. 'I did want to pray for it; but I thought, perhaps, if it was not His Will, I would not—and then what you said. And now He is making it all happy.'

'And you do not grieve over your year of illness?'

'I would not have been without it—no,' said Alfred, very quietly, but with much meaning.

'"It is good for me that I have been in trouble," is what you mean,' said Mr. Cope.

'It has made our Saviour seem—I mean—He is so good to me,' said Alfred fervently.

But talking made him cough, and that brought a line in the fair forehead so full of peace. Mr. Cope would not say more to him, and asked his mother whether the Feast, for which he had so much longed, should be on the following day. She thought it best that it should be so; and Alfred again said, 'Thank you, Sir,' with the serene expression on his face. Mr. Cope read a Psalm and a prayer to him, and thinking him equal to no more, went away, pausing, however, for a little talk with Paul in the shop.

Paul did not say so, but, poor fellow, he had been rather at a loss since Matilda had come. In herself, she was a very good, humble, sensible girl; but she wore a dark silk dress, and looked, moved, and spoke much more like a lady than Ellen: Paul stood in great awe of her, and her presence seemed all at once to set him aloof from the others.

He had been like one of themselves for the last three months, now he felt that he was like a beggar among them; he did not like to call Mrs. King mother, lest it should seem presuming; Ellen seemed to be raised up the same step as her sister, and even Alfred was almost out of his reach; Matilda read to him, and Paul's own good feeling shewed him that he would be only in the way if he spent all his time in Alfred's room as formerly; so he kept down-stairs in the morning, and went to bed very early. Nobody was in the least unkind to him: but he had just begun to grieve at being a burden so long, and to wonder how much longer he should be in getting his health again. And then it might be only to be cast about the world, and to lose his one glimpse of home kindness. Poor boy! he still cried at the thought of how happy Alfred was.

He did all he could to be useful, but he could scarcely manage to stoop down, could carry nothing heavy, and moved very slowly; and he now and then made a dreadful muddle in the shop, when a customer was not like Mrs. Hayward, who told him where everything was, and the price of all she wanted, as well as Mrs. King could do herself. He could sort the letters and see to the post-office very well; and for all his blunders, he did so much by his good-will, that when Mrs. King wanted to cheer him up, she declared that he saved her all the expense of having in a woman from the village to help, and that he did more about the house than Harold.

This was true: for Harold did not like doing anything but manly things, as he called them; whereas Paul did not care what it was, so that it saved trouble to her or Ellen.

Talking and listening to Harold was one use of Paul. Now that it had come upon him, and he saw Alfred worse from day to day, the poor boy was quite broken-hearted. Possibly, when at his work, or riding, he managed to shake off the remembrance; but at home it always came back, and he cried so much at the sight of Alfred, and at any attempt of his brother to talk to him, that they could scarcely let him stay ten minutes in the room. Then, when Paul had gone to bed on the landing at seven o'clock, he would come and sit on his bed, and talk, and cry, and sob about his brother, and his own carelessness of him, often till his mother came out and ordered him down-stairs to his own bed in the kitchen; and Paul turned his face into the pillow to weep himself to sleep, loving Alfred very little less than did his brother, but making less noise about it, and feeling very lonely when he saw how all the family cared for each other.

So Mr. Cope's kind manner came all the more pleasantly to him; and after some talk on what they both most cared about, Mr. Cope said, 'Paul, Mr. Shaw of Berryton tells me he has a capital school-master, but in rather weak health, and he wants to find a good intelligent youth to teach under him, and have opportunities of improving himself. Five pounds a year, and board and lodgings. What do you think of it, Paul?'

Paul's sallow face began growing red, and he polished the counter, on which he was leaning; then, as Mr. Cope repeated, 'Eh, Paul?' he said slowly, and in his almost rude way, 'They wouldn't have me if they knew how I'd been brought up.'

'Perhaps they would if they knew what you've come to in spite of bringing up. And,' added Mr. Cope, 'they are not so much pressed for time but that they can wait till you've quite forgotten your tumble into the Ragglesford. We must fatten you—get rid of those spider-fingers, and you and I must do a few more lessons together—and I think Mrs. King has something towards your outfit; and by Whitsuntide, I told Mr. Shaw that I thought I might send him what I call a very fair sample of a good steady lad.'

Paul did not half seem to take it in—perhaps he was too unhappy, or it sounded like sending him away again; or, maybe, such a great step in life was more than he could comprehend, after the outcast condition to which he had been used: but Mr. Cope could not go on talking to him, for the Grange carriage was stopping at the gate, and Matilda and Ellen were both coming down-stairs to receive Miss Jane. Poor little thing, she looked very pale and nervous; and as she shook hands with the Curate, as he met her in the garden-path, she said with a startled manner, 'Oh! Mr. Cope—were you there? Am I interrupting—?'

'Not at all,' he said. 'I had only called in as I came home, and had just come down again.'

'Is it—is it very dreadful?' murmured Jane, with a sort of gasp. She was so entirely unused to scenes of sadness or pain, that it was very strange and alarming to her, and it was more difficult than ever to believe her no younger than Ellen.

'Very far from dreadful or distressing,' said Mr. Cope kindly, for he knew it was not her fault that she had been prevented from overcoming such feelings, and that this was a great effort of kindness. 'It is a very peaceful, soothing sight—he is very happy, and not in a suffering state.'

'Oh, will you tell Grandmamma?' said Jane, with her pretty look of earnestness; 'she is so much afraid of its much for me, and she was so kind in letting me come.'

So Miss Selby went on to the two sisters, and Mr. Cope proceeded to the carriage, where Lady Jane had put out her head, glad to be able to ask him about the state of affairs. Having nothing but this little grand-daughter left to her, the old lady watched over her with almost over-tender care, and was in much alarm both lest the air of the sick-room should be unwholesome, or the sight too sorrowful for her; and though she was too kind to refuse the wish of the dying boy, she had come herself, in order that 'the child,' as she called her, might not stay longer than was good for her; and she was much relieved to hear Mr. Cope's account of Alfred's calm state, and of the freshness of the clean room, in testimony of which he pointed to the open window.

'Yes,' she said, 'I hope Mary King was wise enough; but I hardly knew how it might be with such a number about the house—that boy and all. He is not gone, is he?'

'No, he is not nearly well enough yet, though he does what he can to be useful to her. When he is recovered, I have a scheme for him.'

So Mr. Cope mentioned Mr. Shaw's proposal, by which my Lady set more store than did Paul as yet. Very kind-hearted she was, though she did not fancy adopting chance-comers into her parish; and as long as he was not saddled upon Mary King, as she said, she was very glad of any good for him; so she told Mr. Cope to come to her for what he might want to fit him out properly for the situation; and turning her keen eyes on him as he stood near the cottage door, pronounced that, after all, he was a nice, decent-looking lad enough, which certainly her Ladyship would not have said before his illness.

Miss Jane did not stay long. Indeed, Alfred could not talk to her, and she did not know what to say to him; she could only stand by his bed, with the tears upon her cheeks, making little murmuring sounds in answer to Mrs. King, who said for her son what she thought he wished to have said. Meanwhile, Jane was earnestly looking at him, remarking with awe, that, changed as he was since she had last seen him—so much more wasted away—the whole look of his face was altered by the gentleness and peace that it had gained, so as to be like the white figure of a saint.

She could not bear it when Mrs. King told her Alfred wanted to thank her for all her kindness in coming to see him. 'Oh, no,' she said, 'I was not kind at all;' and her tears would not be hindered. 'Only, you know, I could not help it.'

Alfred gave her a bright look. Any one could see what a pleasure it was to him to be looking at her again, though he did not repent of his share in the sacrifice for Paul's sake. No, if Paul had been given up that Miss Jane might come to him, Alfred would not have had the training that made all so sweet and calm with him now. He turned his head to the little picture, and said, 'Thank you, Ma'am, for that. That's been my friend.'

'Yes, indeed it has, Miss Jane,' said his mother. 'There's nothing you ever did for him that gave him the comfort that has been.'

'And please, Ma'am,' said Alfred, 'will you tell my Lady—I give her my duty —and ask her pardon for having behaved so bad—and Mrs. Crabbe—and the rest?'

'I will, Alfred; but every one has forgiven that nonsense long ago.'

'It was very bad of me,' said Alfred, pausing for breath; 'and so it was not to mind you—Miss Jane—when you said I was ill for a warning.'

'Did I?' said Jane.

'Yes—in hay-time—I mind it—I didn't mind for long—but 'twas true. He had patience with me.'

The cough came on, and Jane knew she must go; her grandmother had bidden her not to stay if it were so, and she just ventured to squeeze Alfred's hand, and then went down-stairs, checking her tears, to wish Matilda and Ellen good-bye; and as she passed by Paul, told him not to uncover his still very short-haired head, and kindly hoped he was better.

Paul, in his dreary feelings, hardly thought of Mr. Cope's plan, till, as he was getting the letters ready for Harold, he turned up one in Mr. Cope's writing, addressed to the 'Rev. A. Shaw, Berryton, Elbury.'

'That's to settle for me, then,' he said; and Harold who was at tea, asking, 'What's that?' he explained.

'Well,' said Harold, 'every one to his taste! I wouldn't go to school again, not for a hundred pounds; and as to *keeping* school!' (Such a face as he made really caused Paul to smile.) 'Nor you don't half like it, neither,' continued Harold. 'Come, you'd better stay and get work here! I'd sooner be at the plough-tail all day, than poke out my eyes over stuff like that,' pointing to Paul's slate, covered with figures. 'Here, Nelly,' as she moved about, tidying the room, 'do you hear? Mr. Cope's got an offer of a place for Paul—five pounds a year, and board and lodging, to be school-master's whipper-in, or what d'ye call it?'

'What do you say, Harold?' cried Ellen, putting her hands on the back of a chair, quite interested. 'You going away, Paul?'

'Mr. Cope says so—and I must get my living, you know,' said Paul.

'But not yet; you are not well enough yet,' said the kind girl. 'And where did you say—?'

'To Berryton.'

'Berryton—oh! that's just four miles out on the other side of Elbury, where Susan Congleton went to live that was housemaid at the Grange. She says it's such a nice place, and such beautiful organ and singing at church! And what did you say you were to be, Paul?'

'I'm to help the school-master.'

'Gracious me!' cried Ellen. 'Why, such a scholar as you are, you'll be quite a gentleman yet, Paul. Why, they school-masters get fifty or sixty pounds salaries sometimes. I protest it's the best thing I've heard this long time! Was it Mr. Cope's doing, or my Lady's?'

'Mr. Cope's,' said Paul, beginning to think he had been rather less grateful than he ought.

'Ah! it is like him,' said Ellen, 'after all the pains he has taken with you. And you'll not be so far off, Paul: you'll come to see us in the holidays, you know.'

'To be sure he will,' said Harold; 'or if he don't, I shall go and fetch him.'

'Of course he will,' said Ellen, with her hand on Paul's chair, and speaking low and affectionately to console him, as she saw him so downcast; 'don't you know how poor Alfy says he's come to be instead of a son to Mother, and a brother to us? I must go up and tell Alf and mother. They'll be so pleased.'

Paul felt very differently about the plan now. All the house congratulated him upon it, and Matilda evidently thought more of him now that she found he was to have something to do. But such things as these were out of sight beside that which was going on in the room above.

Alfred slept better that night, and woke so much revived, that they thought him better: and Harold, greatly comforted about him, stood tolerably quietly by his side, listening to one or two things that Alfred had longed for months past to say to him.

'Promise me, Harold dear, that you'll be a good son to Mother: you'll be the only one now.'

Harold made a bend of his head like a promise.

'O Harold, be good to her!' went on Alfred earnestly; 'she's had so much trouble! I do hope God will leave you to her—if you are steady and good. Do, Harold! She's not like some, as don't care what their lads get to. And don't take after me, and be idle! Be right-down good, Harold, as Paul is; and when you come to be ill—oh! it won't be so bad for you as it was for me!'

'I do want to be good,' sighed Harold. 'If I'd only been confirmed; but 'twas all along of them merries last summer!'

'And I was such a plague to you—I drove you out,' said Alfred.

'No, no, I was a brute to you! Oh! Alfy, Alfy, if I could only get back the time!'

He was getting to the sobs that hurt his brother; and his sister was going to interfere; but Alfred said:

'Never mind, Harold dear, we've been very happy together, and we'll always love each other. You'll not forget Alf, and you'll be Mother's good son to take care of her! Won't you?'

So Harold gave that promise, and went away with his tears. Poor fellow, now was his punishment for having slighted the Confirmation. Like Esau, an exceeding bitter cry could not bring back what he had lightly thrown away. Well was it for him that this great sorrow came in time, and that it was not altogether his birthright that he had parted with. He found he could not go out to his potato-planting and forget all about it, as he would have liked to have done—something would not let him; and there he was sitting crouched up and sorrowful on the steps of the stairs, when Mr. Cope and all the rest were gathered in Alfred's room, a church for the time. Matilda and Ellen had set out the low table with the fair white cloth, and Mr. Cope brought the small cups and paten, which were doubly precious to him for having belonged to his father, and because the last time he had seen them used had been for his father's last Communion.

Now was the time to feel that a change had really passed over the young pastor in the time of his absence. Before, he could only lead Alfred in his prayers, and give him counsel, tell him to hope in his repentance, and on what that hope was founded. Now that he had bent beneath the hand of the Bishop, he had received, straight down from the Twelve, the Power from on High. It was not Mr. Cope, but the Lord Who had purchased that Pardon by His own most Precious Blood, Who by him now declared to Alfred that the sins and errors of which he had so long repented, were pardoned and taken away. The Voice of Authority now assured him of what he had been only told to hope and trust before. And to make the promise all the more close and certain, here was the means of becoming a partaker of the Sacrifice—here was that Bread and that Cup which shew forth the Lord's Death till He come. It was very great rest and peace, the hush that was over the quiet room, with only Alfred's hurried breath to be heard beside Mr. Cope's voice as he spoke the blessed words, and the low responses of the little congregation. Paul was close beside Alfred—he would have him there between his mother and the wall—and the two whose first Communion it was, were the last to whom Mr. Cope came. To one it was to be the Food for the passage into the unseen world; to the other might it be the first partaking of the Manna to support him through the wilderness of this life.

'From the highways and hedges,' here was one brought into the foretaste of the Marriage Supper. Ah! there was one outside, who had loved idle pleasure when the summons had been sent to him. Perhaps the misery he was feeling now might be the means of sparing him from missing other calls, and being shut out at last.

It seemed to fulfil all that Alfred had wished. He lay still between waking and sleeping for a long time afterwards, and then begged for Paul to read to him the last chapters of the Book of Revelation. Matilda wished to read them for him; but he said, 'Paul, please.' Paul's voice was fuller and softer when it was low; his accent helped the sense, and Alfred was more used to them than to his visitor sister. Perhaps there was still another reason, for when Paul came to the end, and was turning the leaves for one of Alfred's favourite bits, he saw Alfred's eyes on him, as if he wanted to speak. It was to say, 'Brothers quite now, Paul! Thank you. I think God must have sent you to help me.'

Alfred seemed better all the evening, and they went to bed in good spirits; but at midnight, Mr. Cope, who was very deeply studying and praying, the better to fit himself for his new office in the ministry, was just going to shut his book, and go up to bed, when he heard a tremulous ring at the bell.

It was Harold, his face looking very white in the light from Mr. Cope's candle.

'Oh! please, Sir,' he said, 'Alfred is worse; and Mother said, if your light wasn't out, you'd like to know.'

'I am very grateful to her,' said Mr. Cope; and taking up his plaid, he wrapped one end round the boy, and put his arm round him, as he felt him quaking as Paul had done before, but not crying—too much awe-struck for that. He said that his mother thought something had broken in the lungs, and that he would be choked. Mr. Cope made the more haste, that he might judge if the doctor would be of any use.

Paul was sitting up in his bed—they had not let him get up—but his eyes were wide open with distress, as he plainly heard the loud sob that each breath had become. Mrs. King was holding Alfred up in her arms; Matilda was trying to chafe his feet; Ellen was kneeling with her face hidden.

The light of sense and meaning was not gone from Alfred's eyes, though the last struggle had come. He gave a look as though he were glad to see Mr. Cope, and then gazed on his brother. Mrs. King signed to Harold to come nearer, and whispered, 'Kiss him.' His sisters had done so, and he had missed Harold. Then Mr. Cope prayed, and Alfred's eyes at first owned the sounds; but soon they were closed, and the long struggling breaths were all that shewed that the spirit was still there.

'He shall swallow up death in victory, and the Lord God shall wipe away tears from all eyes.'

One moment, and the blue eyes they knew so well were opened and smiling on his mother, and then—

It was over; and through affliction and pain, the young spirit had gone to rest!

The funeral day was a very sore one to Paul Blackthorn. He would have given the world to be there, and have heard the beautiful words of hope which received his friend to his resting-place, but he could not get so far. He had tried to carry a message to a house not half so far off as the church, but his knees seemed to give way under him, and his legs ached so much that he could hardly get home. Somehow, a black suit, just such as Harold's, had come home for him at the same time; but this could not hinder him from feeling that he was but a stranger, and one who had no real place in the home where he lived. There was the house full of people, who would only make their remarks on him—Miss Hardman (who was very critical of the coffin-plate), the school-master, and some of the upper-servants of the house—and poor Mrs. King and Matilda, who could not help being gratified at the attention to their darling, were obliged to go down and be civil to them; while Ellen, less used to restraint, was shut into her own room crying; and Harold was standing on the stairs, very red, but a good deal engaged with his long hat-band. Poor Paul! he had not even his usual refuge—his own bed to lie upon and hide his face—for that had been taken away to make room for the coffin to be carried down.

There, they were going at last, when it had seemed as if the bustle and confusion would never cease. There was Alfred leaving the door where he had so often played, carried upon the shoulders of six lads in white frocks, his old school-fellows and Paul's Confirmation friends. How Paul envied them for doing him that last service! There was his mother, always patient and composed, holding Harold's arm—Harold, who must be her stay and help, but looking so slight, so boyish, and so young, then the two girls, Ellen so overpowered with crying that her sister had to lead her; Mrs. Crabbe with Betsey Hardman, who held up a great white handkerchief, for other people's visible grief always upset her, as she said; and besides, she felt it a duty to cry at such a time; and the rest two and two, quite a train, in their black suits: how unlike the dreary pauper funerals Paul had watched away at Upperscote! That respectable look seemed to make him further off and more desolate, like one cut off, whom no one would follow, no one would weep for. Alfred, who had called him a brother, was gone, and here he was alone!

The others were taking their dear one once more to the church where they had so often prayed that he might have a happy issue out of all his afflictions.

They were met by Mr. Cope, ending his loving intercourse with Alfred by reading out the blessed promise of Resurrection—the assurance that the body they were sowing in weakness would be raised in power; so that the noble boy, whom they had seen fade away like a drooping flower, would rise again blossoming forth in glory, after the Image of the Incorruptible—that Image, thought Mr. Cope, as he read on, which he faithfully strove to copy even through the sufferings due to the corruptible. His voice often shook and faltered. He had never before read that Service; and perhaps, except for those of his own kin, it could never be a greater effort to him, going along with Alfred as he had done, holding up the rod and staff that bore him through the dark valley. And each trembling of his tone seemed to answer something that the mother was feeling in her peaceful, hopeful, thankful grief—yes, thankful that she could lay her once high-spirited and thoughtless boy in his grave, with the same sure and certain hope of a joyful Resurrection, as that ripe and earnest-minded Christian his father, or his little innocent brother. It was peace—awful peace, indeed, but soothing even to Ellen and Harold, new as they were to grief.

But to poor Paul at home, out of hearing of the words of hope, only listening to the melancholy toll of the knell, and quite alone in the disarranged forlorn house, there seemed nothing to take off the edge of misery. He was not wanted to keep Alfred company now, nor to read to him—no one needed him, no one cared for him. He wandered up to where Alfred had lain so long, as if to look for the pale quiet face that used to smile to him. There was nothing but the bed-frame and mattress! He threw himself down on it and cried. He did not well know why—perhaps the chief feeling was that Alfred was gone away to rest and bliss, and he was left alone to be weary and without a friend.

At last the crying began to spend itself, and he turned and looked up. There was Alfred's little picture of the Crucified still on the wall, and the words under it, 'For us!' Paul's eye fell on it; and somehow it brought to mind what Alfred had said to him on Christmas Day. There was One Who had no home on earth; there was One Who had made Himself an outcast and a wanderer, and Who had not where to lay His Head. Was not He touched with a fellow-feeling for the lonely boy? Would He not help him to bear his friendless lot as a share of His own Cross? Nay, had He not raised him up friends already in his utmost need? 'There is a Friend Who sticketh closer than a brother.' He was the Friend that Paul need never lose, and in Whom he could still meet his dear Alfred. These thoughts, not quite formed, but something like them, came gently as balm to the poor boy, and though they brought tears even thicker than the first burst of lonely sorrow, they were as peaceful as those shed beside the grave. Though Paul was absent in the body, this was a very different shutting out from Harold's on last Tuesday.

Paul must have cried himself to sleep, for he did not hear the funeral-party return, and was first roused by Mrs. King coming up-stairs. He had been so much used to think of this as Alfred's room, that he had never recollected that it was hers; and now that she was come up for a moment's breathing-time, he started up ashamed and shocked at being so caught.

But good motherly Mrs. King saw it all, and how he had been weeping where her child had so long rested. Indeed, his face was swelled with crying, and his voice all unsteady.

'Poor lad! poor lad!' she said kindly, 'you were as fond of him as any of them; and if we wanted anything else to make you one of us, that would do it.'

'O Mother,' said Paul, as she kindly put her hand on him, 'I could not bear it —I was so lost—till I looked at *that*,'pointing to the little print.

'Ay,' said Mrs. King, as she wiped her quiet tears, 'that Cross was Alfred's great comfort, and so it is to us all, my boy, whatever way we have to carry it, till we come to where he is gone. No cross, no crown, they say.'

Perhaps it was not bad for any one that this forlorn day had given Paul a fresh chill, which kept him in bed for nearly a week, so as gently to break the change from her life of nursing to Mrs. King, and make him very happy and peaceful in her care.

And when at last on a warm sunny Sunday, Paul Blackthorn returned thanks in church for his recovery—ay, and for a great deal besides—he had no reason to think that he was a stranger cared for by no one.

CHAPTER XIII—SIX YEARS LATER

It is a beautiful morning in Easter week. The sun is shining on the gilded weathercock, which flashes every time it veers from south to west; the snowdrops are getting quite out of date, and the buttercups and primroses have it all their own way; the grass is making a start, and getting quite long upon the graves in Friarswood churchyard.

'Really, I should have sent in the Saxon monarch to tidy us up!' says to himself the tall young Rector, as he stepped over the stile with one long stride; 'but I suppose he is better engaged.'

That tall young Rector is the Reverend Marcus Cope, six years older, but young still. The poor old Rector, Mr. John Selby, died four years ago abroad; and Lady Jane and Miss Selby's other guardians gave the living to Mr. Cope, to the great joy of all the parish, except the Shepherds, who have never forgiven him for their own usage of their farming boy, nor for the sermon he neither wrote nor preached.

The Saxon monarch means one Harold King, who looks after the Rectory garden and horse, as well as the post-office and other small matters.

The clerk is unlocking the church, and shaking out the surplice, and Mr. Cope goes into the vestry, takes out two big books covered with green parchment, and sees to the pen. It is a very good one, judging by the writing of the last names in that book. They are Francis Mowbray and Jane Arabella Selby.

'Captain and Mrs. Mowbray will be a great blessing to the place, if they go on as they have begun,' thinks Mr. Cope. 'How happy they are making old Lady Jane, and how much more Mrs. Mowbray goes among the cottages now that she does more as she pleases.'

Then Mr. Cope goes to the porch and looks out. He sees two men getting over the stile. One is a small slight person, in very good black clothes, not at all as if they were meant to ape a gentleman, and therefore thoroughly respectable. He has a thin face, rather pointed as to the chin and nose, and the eyes dark and keen, so that it would be over-sharp but that the mouth looks so gentle and subdued, and the whole countenance is grave and thoughtful. You could not feel half so sure that he is a certificated school-master, as you can that his very brisk-looking companion is so.

'Good morning, Mr. Brown.—Good morning, Paul,' said Mr. Cope. 'I did not expect to see you arrive in this way.'

157

The grave face glitters up in a merry look of amusement, while, with a little colouring, he answers:

'Why, Sir, Matilda said it was the proper thing, and so we supposed she knew best.'

There are not so many people who *do* talk of Paul now. Most people know him as Mr. Blackthorn, late school-master at Berryton, where the boys liked him for his bright and gentle yet very firm ways; the parents, for getting their children on, and helping them to be steady; and the clergyman, for being so perfectly to be trusted, so anxious to do right, and, while efficient and well informed, perfectly humble and free from conceit. Now he has just got an appointment to Hazleford school, in another diocese, with a salary of fifty pounds a year; but, as Charles Hayward would tell you, 'he hasn't got one bit of pride, no more than when he lived up in the hay-loft.'

There is not long to wait. There is another party getting over the stile. There is a very fine tall youth first. As Betsey Hardman tells her mother, 'she never saw such a one for being fine-growed and stately to look at, since poor Charles King when he wore his best wig.' A very nice open honest face, and as merry a pair of blue eyes as any in the parish, does Harold wear, nearly enough to tell you that, if in these six years it would be too much to say he has never done *anything* to vex his mother, yet in the main his heart is in the right place—he is a very good son, very tender to her, and steady and right-minded.

Whom is he helping over the stile? Oh, that is Mrs. Mowbray's pretty little maid! a very good young thing, whom she has read with and taught; and here, lady-like and delicate-looking as ever, is Matilda. Bridemaids before the bride! that's quite wrong; but the bride has a shy fit, and would not get over first, and Matilda and Harold are, the one encouraging her, the other laughing at her; and Mr. Blackthorn turns very red, and goes down the path to meet her, and she takes his arm, and Harold takes Lucy, and Mr. Brown Miss King.

Very nice that bride looks, with her hair so glossy under her straw bonnet trimmed with white, her pretty white shawl, and quiet purple silk dress, her face rather flushed, but quiet-looking, as if she were growing more like her mother, with something of her sense and calmness.

How Mr. Blackthorn ever came to ask her that question, nobody can guess, and Harold believes he does not know himself. However, it got an answer two years ago, and Mrs. King gave her consent with all her heart, though she knew Betsey Hardman would talk of picking a husband up out of the gutter, and that my Lady would look severe, and say something of silly girls. Yes— and though the rich widower bailiff had said sundry civil things of Miss Ellen being well brought up and notable—'For,' as Mrs. King wrote to Matilda, 'I had rather see Ellen married to a good religious man than to any one, and I do not know one I can be so sure of as Paul, nor one that is so like a son to me; and if he has no friends belonging to him, that is better than bad friends.' And Ellen herself, from looking on him as a mere boy, as she had done at their first acquaintance, had come to thinking no one ever had been so wise or so clever, far less so good, certainly not so fond of her—so her answer was no great wonder. Then they were to be prudent, and wait for some dependence; and so they did till Mr. Shaw recommended Paul Blackthorn for Hazleford school, where there is a beautiful new house for the master, so that he will have no longer to live in lodgings, and be 'done for,' as the saying is. Harold tells Ellen that he is afraid that without her he won't wash above once in four months; but however that may be, she is convinced that the new school-house will be lost on him, and that in spite of all his fine arithmetic, his fifty pounds will never go so far for one as for two; and so she did not turn a deaf ear to his entreaties that she would not send him alone to Hazleford.

They wanted very much to get 'Mother' to come and live with them, give up the post-office, and let Harold live in Mr. Cope's house; but Mother has a certain notion that Harold's stately looks and perfect health might not last, if she were not always on the watch to put him into dry clothes if he comes in damp, and such like 'little fidgets,' as he calls them, which he would not attend to from any one but Mother. So she will keep on the shop and the post-office, and try to break in that uncouth girl of John Farden's to be a tidy little maid; and Mr. and Mrs. Blackthorn will spend their holidays with her and Harold. She may come to them yet in time, if, as Paul predicts, Master Harold takes up with Lucy at the Grange—but there's time enough to think of that; and even if he should, it would take many years to make Lucy into such a Mrs. King as she who is now very busy over the dinner at home, but thinking about a good deal besides the dinner.

There! Paul and Ellen have stood and knelt in an earnest reverent spirit, making their vows to one another and before God, and His blessing has been spoken upon them to keep them all their lives through.

It is with a good heart of hope that Mr. Cope speaks that blessing, knowing that, as far as human eye can judge, here stands a man who truly feareth the Lord, and beside him a woman with the ornament of a meek and quiet spirit.

They are leaving the church now, the bridegroom and his bride, arm in arm, but they turn from the path to the wicket, and Harold will not let even Matilda follow them. Just by the south wall of the church there are three graves, one a very long one, one quite short, one of middle length. The large one has a head-stone, with the names of Charles King, aged forty years, and Charles King, aged seven years. The middle-sized one has a stone cross, and below it

'Alfred King, aged sixteen years,' and the words, 'In all their afflictions He was afflicted.'

It was Matilda who paid the cost of that stone, Miss Selby who drew the pattern of it, and 'Mother' who chose the words, as what Alfred himself loved best. At the bottom of Ellen's best work-box is a copy of verses about that very cross. She thinks they ought to have been carved out upon it, but Paul knows a great deal better, so all she could do was to write them out on a sheet of note-paper with a wide lace border, and keep them as her greatest treasure. Perhaps she prizes them even more than the handsome watch that Mr. Shaw gave Paul, though less, of course, than the great Bible and Prayer-book, in which Mr. Cope has waited till this morning to write the names of Paul and Ellen Blackthorn.

So they stand beside the cross, and read the words, and they neither of them can say anything, though the white sweet face is before the eyes of their mind at the same time, and Ellen thinks she loves Paul twice as much for having been one of his great comforts.

'Good-bye, Alfred dear,' she whispers at last.

'No, not good-bye,' says Paul. 'He is as much with us as ever, wherever we are. Remember how we were together, Ellen. I have always thought of him at every Holy Communion since, and have felt that if till now, no one living— at least one at rest, were mine by right.'

Ellen pressed his arm.

'Yes,' said Paul; 'the months I spent with Alfred were the great help and blessing of my life. I don't believe any recollection has so assisted to guard me in all the frets and temptations there are in a life like mine.'